CW00494712

No Spider Harmed in the Making of This Book

EDITED BY

Cherry Potts

ARACHNE PRESS

First published in UK 2020 by Arachne Press Limited
100 Grierson Road, London SE23 1NX
www.arachnepress.com

ISBNs
Print 978-1-909208-93-3
ePub 978-1-909208-94-0
Mobi/kindle 978-1-909208-95-7

Thanks to Muireann Grealy for her proofing.
Thanks to Karen Boissonneault-Gauthier for her cover design
Printed on wood-free paper in the UK by TJ International, Padstow.

Contents

No Spider Harmed in the Making of This Book

This book is dedicated to
Lady Hale, and her spider brooch
(UK Supreme Court, 24th September 2019)

Introduction

Cherry Potts

Eight years ago, when I started Arachne Press, I was searching for a suitable name, and came up with a short-list of five – I wanted something that felt like it had some history, and a strong female statement of intent. I sent that list of five to everyone I knew who had anything to do with publishing – authors, creative writing tutors, librarians, publishers, printers… opinion was fairly evenly divided, but then someone came back saying *anything but Arachne, because I hate spiders, and other people who hate spiders won't buy the books;* and I thought *Really? Really??* and being of a contrary nature, that made up my mind for me. Arachne was on the list in the first place because we wanted our website to be integral, and because as a writer myself I often use spinning and weaving as a metaphor *in* my writing and as a metaphor *for* writing; and because one of my very first published stories was *Arachne's Daughters* which is a lecture given by a spider (probably in semaphore) at an archive meeting of the Arachno-Lesbian league, thirteen years after the revolution…

Fast forward seven years and watching the historic judgement of the Supreme Court in rejecting the legality of the prorogation of Parliament, I was entranced by Lady Hale's spider brooch, and texted my partner, who was outside the court, *It's going to be alright, she's wearing a spider.* A completely illogical response, but as I turned off the TV and went back to my desk I thought, *Time for a spider anthology,* and *Oh! It's our eighth anniversary next August!*

I was not expecting many stories or poems, and was resigned to publishing a slim volume of eight poems and eight stories, and possibly including *Arachne's Daughters*, but no! This was the biggest response we've ever had to a call-out, despite my strictures to avoid horror, and that no spider should die; except, perhaps, heroically.

So thank you to all those writers who upheld my faith in human nature, and thank you to Lady Hale for inadvertantly giving me the nudge to celebrate spiders properly.

Poems

Moonlight is Web-Coloured

Emma Lee

(female ladybird spiders weave tunnel webs)

His scarlet back
brightened the night
of a crescent moon,
just visible from my tunnel
in the dry pale earth.
His feet plucked our tune.
Spiderlings shift in their eggs.
I parcel prey.
Hope they understand.
Spiderlings fidget.
I will purge food
as the sun sands
the earth, give them
the best chance I can.

recluse

Eugene Goldin

she distanced from her friends upon learning, from a Gypsy, that in a previous life she had been a brown recluse spider – this information helped her to understand her love of closed, dark places where an innocent soul might wander – unexpectedly – looking for a treat or an adventure – you know those spaces – we all have them – some are known as pride – others – self-stimulation – and that's where she lived – behind the stairs – in a solitary basement – hiding from direct illumination – like a prayer in an abandoned orphanage – or sunlight's slant slashed through the drapes of a funeral parlour – under the floor boards – where, if you lose your way – your eyes might meet hers, darkly.

Spider Queen

Jennifer Rood

Spiders sense the signal: October nights
turned cold. It is time for the invasions.
My ten-year-old sentinel guards our realm
tonight. She calls me from sleep, announcing:
There's a REALLY big spider in my room.
Dreams scatter like dry leaves, and I am up,
ready to confront this foreign queen. Oh,
she is magnificent when I see her!

Hairy, black, and muscular, she is thick,
an eight-legged gorilla, a rare beast,
and beautiful in the regal tulle of
the shimmering silver Barbie ball gown
she has climbed into. I survey the scene.
She has the high ground, a purple pillow
upon which she is poised both for attack
or retreat, but I have the advantage.

I move first, testing her resolve, tapping
the pillow. She is quick and aggressive,
darting forward to meet her foe. But it
is a bluff, and she holds her position,
advancing no farther. *I may have to*
kill her, I think, but I prefer exile
and banishment. After all, she is a
creature like me. Perhaps this is weakness.

I will never earn her friendship; she will
not sit like Charlotte and weave words into
her webs over my bed. SOME HUMAN or
TERRIFIC will never appear. But she
is SOME SPIDER, RADIANT, and so I
think a bit longer before I decide,
then pick up the pillow, take her outside,
and bid her good luck in that October night.

Spider Haiku

Hugh Findlay

Forgive me spider –
The business of your web
  Shaken by my hand

Spider

Elizabeth Ditty

too many nimble
legs knitting silk and nightmares
spinning gentle deaths

Spin

Kate Foley

is the Dutch word for spider
and *spin* it does, running out
a miniature steel hawser
mooring small creatures
to its dangerous harbour.

Spin,
as days do and their small
cousins, minutes and seconds that tumble
from a basket of hours.

What if they won't?
What if they cluster
and clutter, a bundle
of grey hairs, threads
from a net of dreams?

What if they wriggle
and fidget like veins
on the hills of old hands?

'Bah!'
'Twist them round your fingers
and wind into the strong red
rope of memory!'
says that strict governess,
Time.

Conversation, September Garden

Chris Cantu

I remember the day you recognised
me – the soft white spider
lodged in the lily's throat.
You were digging in the earth
but then stopped and leaned
against your shovel – hello.

For a long time we spoke
silently about my body, the way
it perfectly matched the creaminess
of the petals, except my one leg
where it brushed the stamen;
there I was painted pollen-yellow.

I knew you then as one
who speaks a language that swings
like a gate on easy hinges, now my way
now yours.
I was marvellous and you,
you were the one who saw me shining.

The Industry of Spiders

Tricia Knoll

The Industry of Spiders
Vans rolls up blazoned
with graphics touting
eco-friendliness, names like alpha and omega.
We eliminate pests!

(People who write in library books
or fail to scoop dog poop?
Overbearing talk-radio hosts?
People who preach at my front door?)

These vans are about bugs.
Men in green t-shirts flaunt tanks
and wands. (Do women do this job?)
They walk perimeters, spraying cracks.
I'm tempted by good riddance
to carpenter ants and yellow jackets.

The sales representative knocks.
He will let me join my neighbours,
a reduced cost to get the spiders.

'Where there are spiders,
there are bugs for them to eat.'
Did he get a face full of orb web
on his way here, between the maple and the
rhododendron?

He's practiced his speech
about chemical safety and pest nests.
His words smack my morning in the garden:
tiny ants scurrying beneath logs I pried apart,
rushing eggs to safety; potato pill bugs
hustling in my compost, shiny dung beetles
I surprised preparing for daffodils.
Everybody has something to do
before winter comes.
I close the door, nicely.
The van and man roll on.

The Matter of the Metta Bhavanna

Seth Crook

'Lie back,
get comfortable,
visualise',
she tells the class.

And so to the image of myself,
on a foam mat,
socks still on,
to wish myself well.

And then the image of a friend,
turning to me,
telling me how her pigs are.
Wish a friend well.

Then somebody I barely know:
the wife of the grumpy crofter,
Mr Circles-In-His-Tractor.
Wish Mrs thingy well.

May her husband,
one muddy pre-Spring,
run away with his true love,
or at least chug off.

Then the difficult person.
Wish them well,
or at least try.
If you fail, try again.

Imagine them in the rain,
standing at a bus stop
ten pence short of the bus fare,
not yet knowing.

Think: May they thrive.
May their rain stop.
May they enjoy
their long walk home.

Stage Five. The Big Band.
Combine the quartet
with all sentient beings everywhere,
wish every band member well.

Let the chorus swell.
Cultivate a wider love.
Help it ripen.
Be the greater hug.

But I am still on a rug
(under the mat of the metta).

The car alarm outside is a distraction.
'Accept it', she says in soft,
but determined voice.
'Think of it as a difficult person'.

We all wish it well.
May it be free of suffering.
May it know peace.
May nobody have broken in.

But it keeps going.
May it know peace.
It keeps going. It keeps going.
May we know peace.

We're still on our backs,
Six months ago, nobody checked the ceiling.
Now we've all wished a greater happiness
on the spider in the corner.

May it know its webby kind of joy.
May it hammock, contented,
although keen to trap and eat some creature.
We wish the spider well, we wish the creature ill.

No,
we wish the creature well,
we wish the spider ill.
No, we wish them both well...

...and hear another car alarm,
further down the street,
from the other side of the argument,
a grating counterpoint.

'Difficult people often come in pairs'
she says, in a soft
but still determined voice.
'Anger breeds anger'.

We wish them both well,
combine them
with all car alarms everywhere,
wish them all well.
Let everything avoid being eaten
at least for a while.

Courtship
Mark Andrew Heathcote

It was all so natural
somehow we forget
you know courtship
like a spider's web
requires a sacrifice
a degree of patience
but most of all
in a relationship,
shouldn't we be, well?
Open and receptive
enough to forgive
break all that tension
and willing to start again.

Gifted

Joanne L.M. Williams

I'm crowned the greatest weaver now.
My workroom is the olive tree;
my loom is formed from branch and bough;
my thread the finest you will see.
Eight dextrous legs outmatch two arms
to go about my artistry,
the best of all the countless charms
found in this form she gifted me.

My body, dark and velvety,
the grey-eyed wisdom goddess gave
Arachne not for blasphemy,
but as reward, from death to save.
This shape permits me to be free:
the silk spun with eternal skill
depicts my mortal history.
I'm crowned the greatest weaver. Still.

Femmes Fatales
Stella Wulf

Be fearless, my mother always said,
it takes more than long legs
and fine bones, to get on in life.
She showed me how to draw a line
between courage and bravado,
a slight aimed at my father,
a common or garden sort,
overawed by her audacity.
I watched him eaten up by it.

Insatiable, as children are, I fed on her
scriptures, learned to push boundaries,
abseil the steepest inclines,
bivouac on precipitous planes,
to sling my hammock over the abyss,
with courage, dexterity and finesse.

But for all my prowess, I find
it is lust that captivates a man.
A slip of silk clings to the body,
inflames him, sets his heart racing,
turns him into a quivering jelly.
Such power is intoxicating.

Sometimes, I leave them dangling,
weak creatures that they are,
just to see them squirm.
And when they're subdued,
I cocoon them in a false
sense of security.

My biggest thrill is to watch them sleep,
to spin my dreams through their hair,
skitter light as air over closed lids,
lashes silky as spiderlings,
to pause on the lip, feel the breath
of air hushing from the moist cave
of an open mouth,
to step fearlessly into the dark.

If You Kill a Spider, the Rain Will Come

Natalie Rowe

After my father died
a spider chose a corner
of our doorway to spin
her autumn web, snaring
the last of the moths
beating against the light.
I began to talk to her
wishing her a good hunt
as I headed to work,
admiring her mummified catch
when I returned at night.
In her silken abbey, the spider
dined without comment
then snipped the lines and let
her quarry's husks
spiral to the floor.
I admired her patience
and cat-like ways,
but I began to worry
as the days shortened
and wood smoke
infused the night, because
I could not stand to lose
one more living thing.

So I threw houseflies at her web
and watched her scurry
down a radial
to fang a free meal.
And while I had no sympathy
for the hapless blue bottles,
I had a world of it for her,
and I started to think
I could keep her going
through an entire Montreal winter
maybe throwing in
a cockroach or two
attracted by my slob of a neighbour.
But one raw morning
I came out to her empty web,
tattered and waiting for the repairs
that would never come,
and I opened my hand
to set her breakfast free.

Lady Hale
Jennifer A. McGowan

Spider silk is
strong as steel
and tougher than Kevlar.

Sometimes
it is the only thing
holding the world
together

and the only protein
that sustains it.

Mayday

Daisy Bassen

May 6, 2018

The old spider died,
Finally, though we didn't know
We were waiting for it,
Not the way disloyal courtiers,
Painted eyes cast up to a heaven
Full of saints on the payroll,
Must have prayed, devoutly,
For the end of Louis XI.
This spider was a lady, old school,
Only in print for her funeral.
No one marked the day of her birth.
She was ordinary then, miss-ish
About her burrow. She worked in silk
And mud; Louis, also called Prudent,
Chose treaties, assignations, marriage,
He stole his father's pet – it doesn't matter.
They'll both be logged on Wikipedia,
Succeeded by offspring, half-alive in code.

Ms Muffet Considers her Options

Sarah Lawson

Little Miss Muffet
sat on a tuffet
watching a spider
because all afternoon
she had been thinking
of becoming a biologist.

The little arthropod
was building a net
for flies to trawl themselves into.

The spider, small and leggy,
had made a labour-saving device
to obtain leisure for other pursuits.
If she acquired a surplus of flies
she could establish trade relations
with other spiders.
Wholesale flies for cheaper meals,
then rental webs and franchise deals.

Little Miss Muffet was changing
to economics
and leaning towards the LSE
when her mother
called her in for tea.

Money Spider

Tracy Davidson

a money spider
skitters across my loose change
and notes on haiku

its miniscule legs
trace seventeen syllables
quicker than I do

I could write an ode
about the gossamer threads
he leaves behind him

but words, like cobwebs,
are best served in small doses
and soon disappear

Arachne in Bloom: An Evocation

Federica Santini

If raising your soft, woven head
or stating your worth in silver
calls for revenge, the sudden twang
of senses enhanced, your glossy fingers
twisted on much smoother thread, then
eat up that pain and revel in the novel,
elongated limbs of velvety charcoal,
nimbler than the injured thread you held
as proof of your last restless night.

Bathe in the reflected light of a myriad
new knots, sense the unknown textures
of woven silver twirled along your
elegant joints, feel the smooth gilded
coin of the sun steadying your firm
jaws, your womb prideful, swollen
with life by the hundreds. Rise.

Savour your own new scent of
growing leaves and limbs as permanent
as the roots where you stepped, a virgin.

Sense your prey. Rise. Lift up your
translucent head, the twisted tangle
of hair muted, eyes open to this new
world, steady your step as you walk into
nature reversed and renewed, aslosh with
truth. If punishment comes as a gift,
shame forgone and rules eaten up,
if it's penance, this smoky velvet of skin,
rise, woman, no more as yourself
but as the truer you/her, as she who was you
before and will be now and always.

This is the place in the blizzard, the
time when you never come back.

Rise, Arachne, in bloom.

Wake to your new thread. Rise.

Stories

Spiders I Have Known

Martha Nance

1

Tiny jumping spider on a red zinnia petal four-eyeing me carefully as I move ever closer with my giant cyclopic camera. He rises and puffs himself up threateningly to a full quarter inch size lookinglookinglookinglooking me in the eye until suddenly he

drops to some invisible spot on the ground, gone, safe. Photoshoot over.

2

Stickydust cobwebs in the corner of the barn, and, well, maybe even the corners of the guest bedroom and of course those shelves in the garage with stuff on them untouched by humans for at least ten years. I just hope that these aren't the homes of brown recluse spiders, or black widow spiders (do they make webs? cobwebs? nests?) And by the way, does anyone ever actually see a spider associated with a cobweb? Is there any such thing as a new cobweb, or are they are born old and draping and dusty?

3

Daddy long legs in the cellar, and out in the woods. 'Are they spiders, or are they just insects? How can you tell?'

'Think,' earthly-wise twelve-year-old I say to my nature-deprived, apartment-dwelling cousins – 'there is a simple answer to that question. Start counting legs, and if you get to eight, which you will, then it must be a…'

'Spider?' the older one guesses, after a too-long pause.

'Yes! And they aren't even poisonous.' Off we gallop happily on our nature hunt.

4

Then there are those spiders that, at least in Minnesota, live only in glass houses, at the pet store, or zoo, big hairy guys that I used to confuse with Dracula, and later on, half jokingly, with an actor named Tarantino. How many other words do you know that end with 'ula', or start with 'tarant'? I have never felt particularly close to a tarantula, nor have a desire to see one in its natural home.

5

But native to my front yard field, in great numbers, are the orb-weavers, the Argiopes. In August, their beautiful foot-tall spirals catch the dew and reflect the early morning sun in great numbers between the thistles and goldenrods and spikes of field grass. These colorful spiders work all evening, perfecting their spokes and spirals, measuring silk in spiderfoot lengths, then unabashedly signing their works right in the middle with their own signature latticework. Today's model is waiting in mid-web, each foot poised on a different silk strand, waiting for the vibrations that tell her the rising sun has delivered a careless early riser to her for breakfast – perhaps a sleepy grasshopper, or a young dragonfly. I wait with her, camera in hand. Suddenly, she has captured a green darner, a major feast. Like any other hunter, she is not merciful when it comes to breakfast. She kills efficiently, ruthlessly, and encloses her meal in silk wrap to keep it fresh.

Does she pause at any point to admire the artistry of her

nightwork? I don't think so. It is left to me to declare it to be beautiful and show it to you, or for you to walk out into the field yourself.

6

Eight worlds, or let's call them countries, each a spider foot delicately positioned on a web, and each foot containing thousands or millions of sensors, humans like you and me. One could wish for eight eyes' worth of clear vision between the feet, as the Argiopes have. But instead, like nerves in the foot of the spider, we detect unthinkingly the slightest movement in the web that connects us, and respond instantly and abundantly when we feel a change. Like those individual nerves, although we record and react to tiny changes in our environment, we forget – or have no capacity to know? – that with the movement of each spider foot, each country or world, the whole web shudders.

More questions: What do we trap in our world-web? Is our large spiderous self, itself, living in a Dracutino house, to the amusement of some larger being? Are we poisonous? Do we reside in a neglected corner of a larger universe with other cobwebbed worlds, sticky with dust? Is it possible for us, unlike the Argiope, to recognize beauty in our web? I ask my cousin, the artist, and my other cousin, the scientist, these questions, but they disagree, so I ask you.

I am pretty sure, however, that our worlds and countries do not share the jumping spider's luxury of falling instantly to an invisible safe spot.

Spidergirl

Margaret Crompton

We were sisters. Twins. Born on the eighth day of the eighth month of the eighth year after our Mother's term as Year Queen. From the start, our limbs were long and slender and very flexible. Mother would laugh and call us her Spidergirl. Girl. Not girls. She was firm. Did it take both of us to make one whole person? Just because four arms and four legs add up to eight. We each managed perfectly well with our own allocation of two of each kind.

She'd never tell who had come first. Most twins, we were sure, were born consecutively. But Mother's smooth face would transform into a web of smiley wrinkles as she assured us that we'd been concurrent. Floated into the world on silken parachutes, she'd laugh. My Spidergirl. We had no one to ask, to explain what would have constituted a natural birth. For anyone. Certainly not for a Spidergirl.

At school, we both excelled. We were unbeatable gymnasts. Running, climbing, hanging upside-down from wall-bars, balancing on narrow beams, swinging on ropes. We could hide in spaces smaller than the actual volume of our supple bodies.

Our other great talent was for craftwork. Other children struggled to thread needles, pricking soft fingers and trailing bloodspots across clean linen. Others ravelled wool into imploding balls, or embroidered unconvincing flowers onto fraying samplers.

It was the custom for the oldest girl in The School to be Year Queen. A great honour. Instead of the close-fitting black uniform, she would wear a white dress, freshly laundered every day. Her hair would be loose, instead of tiny plaits so tight that they made your head ache. She would dance and write poetry, take the lead in the school play, and sing solo in concerts.

In our year, we were the oldest girl. 'But no,' insisted Headteacher. 'You are two separate girls. Only one of you can be Year Queen. Ask your Mother who is the elder.'

Mother's face was as covered with smiley wrinkles as when we first asked who had been born first. 'Concurrent,' she confirmed, laconic as ever. 'Con. Current. It means, *running*, or in your case *borning, together*.' She enjoyed her own joke. We did not.

Because we had been born concurrently, we were precluded from ever becoming Year Queen, whether concurrently or consecutively.

We consulted Miss Anansi, a famously ruthless lawyer, already fabulously rich and successful. As former Year Queen herself, she understood our grave predicament. In an essentially competitive society, every girl needed a sackful of assets, qualifications, glowing references, admiring reviews, invitations and opportunities. Above all, the wonderful prospects of a Year Queen.

One year. One Queen. Not twins. One twin alone, not a concurrent pair.

But there was a mystery. When her year ended, the Queen had one final duty. She was required to marry. Although not her boyfriend or the man of her dreams, her husband would be 'The Perfect Match,' we were always told. And that was all we were told. Only the retiring Year Queen would learn the secret, on the day after she left school.

Even feisty Miss Anansi wouldn't break that silence. But she hatched a plan. If we refused, we would be expelled, and no other girl of our family ever admitted to The School. Of course we accepted. Whatever happened, we'd still be – Spidergirl.

Even if one of us served a year in luxury, while the other drudged, second-best. Only. One. Year.

Once we'd agreed, Miss Anansi explained her plan to identify Spidergirl's temporarily-senior half. Obvious really, in such a competitive society. A competition. 'We can do that,' we assured ourselves. 'We cannot be divided. Whoever is judged to have won, we are still one.' Note: 'Whoever is judged to have won.' Not 'Whoever wins'. We could not conceive that either of us would be described as 'the winner'.

Headteacher was, simply, relieved that the problem had been – or at least would be – solved. Mother had lost interest. She was pregnant again. There would be more daughters, more Year Queen candidates. Consecutive or concurrent? Not her worry. Her job was conceiving, bearing, borning.

Miss Anansi organised the competition in two parts, to give each of us an equal chance. First, craft. A classroom was divided in half by painted paper screens. Each half was filled with identical materials – wool, silk, canvas; wood, wicker, cane. There were shuttles, needles and bobbins; looms, tambours and frames; spinning-wheels and spindles, potters' wheels and clay. Buffets were laden with light refreshments. Younger girls were deputed to keep us supplied with materials, and arrange completed work on display stands. We were content. We had no need to see each other to be together.

We were informed that Judges were hidden behind a curtain whose embroidery depicted a decorously-draped man deciding on which of three equally-beautiful totally naked women he would bestow the prize of an apple. The Judges would watch how we worked, and ensure that we couldn't cheat. We were shocked, offended that anyone could imagine we'd think of cheating. Let alone not only *think* of cheating, but actually cheat.

The competition comprised three tasks. No surprise there.

What worthwhile contest had ever demanded more, or fewer, than three achievements? We must first use wool, then silk, and finally we could choose whatever we wished, provided that we had never before used the material. And we must create first a picture, then some piece of equipment; the final choice must be an experiment, something we had never before attempted. We were keen to begin.

We each created a picture with a kaleidoscope of fine wools. One was embroidered on bleached canvas stretched taut on a wooden frame, needles flashing. Icarus soars to the sun on wings crafted from eagle's feathers stitched into hardened wax, then falls to his death through the sea where he lies forever on the sandy bed, his oblivious father flying on, his mother waiting on the shore he will never reach. Earth, air, fire, water, and earth again.

One was woven on a great loom, plain warp supporting a thousand weft threads, shuttle shining. Penelope is creating her panorama of Odysseus's cruise through leisurely encounters with Nausicaa, Circe, Sirens, which she weaves through the day and unpicks through the night to deceive the predatory suitors who seek not her devotion but her power. Imagination, endurance, love, all maintained by courage.

Our chosen themes were ancient, universal, but we set the people in our own time, our own places, unlike the Arcadian embroidered apple-man with his unclothed goddesses. Icarus's mother mourns on the beach beside our city, while Penelope weaves in the room where we ourselves were working.

Next, we twined and braided lengths of silk rope, some with decorative bands or ribbon insertions, all unbreakable, strong enough to bear the greatest weight. We made belts and coils, skipping ropes and rugs, sandals and sunhats.

Finally, we experimented with our personal choices. Although there was plenty of material and equipment, we found nothing we had never before used. We waited to become clear, sitting in silence with folded hands. We each became ready in the same moment. One of us began to sing, without words, a melody which no one had ever heard. The other began to clap a rhythm no one had ever felt. *Lament of the Mourning Mother. Ballad of the Waiting Wife.*

What could the Judges do? Prefer the essential elements of physical life to the spiritual? Choose the bereaved mother or the faithful wife? Our tapestries were both perfect. Our ropes faultless. Our music beyond words. The Judges remained behind their embroidered curtain, sending their messenger, Iris, to inform us of their decision. We had, she reported, demonstrated through the perfection of our craft and the narratives we had selected, that each was complete in herself, yet also essential to the other. There was – there could be – no winner. When we were free to talk to each other, we wondered whether anyone had noticed our silent comment on the apple-man and his un-clad contestants?

Next day, however, must decide the dilemma, one way or another. They meant, one sister or another. The Judges still deluded themselves that we two who were one could be divided. The gymnastics competition comprised three tasks. Naturally. We were locked into the fully equipped gymnasium from which we would be freed only when one of us had won. One to stride out in triumph as Year Queen. One to sidle out in humiliation as – who would care? For the first time in our life, we felt nervous. But we had never declined a challenge. And we never would. Iris was still speaking: Points would be awarded for agility, courage, flexibility... We stopped listening as the list lengthened. Lists and points were irrelevant to the challenge we set for ourselves.

First came climbing. We chose the bars which lined the gymnasium like prison walls. We reached the top in less than a second and stood on one leg – one left, one right. She of the left scuttled in that direction, while the other went to the right. With perfect timing, we met at our starting point. As shimmering streamers unwound from our waists and floated like gossamers, we circumnavigated the room again, this time descending one section of bars diagonally, then ascending the next in the same way until, again, coinciding perfectly at the starting/finishing point. Now we set off again, hanging from the top bar, moving hand-over-hand, faster and faster.

Until suddenly, we leapt to the rope. One rope. One leap. Four hands perfectly placed, left holding left, right holding right. Neither of us lower on the rope. Or higher. Now, holding on with our feet, we bent backwards to grasp other ropes, two each. We dropped the first rope and delighted in a display of ropewomanship, climbing and swinging, swooping and coiling, flying to each other's rope and returning to our own.

Then turning topsy-turvy, we descended head-first to the floor where, at once, we were dancing. Our own dance. *Lament of the Mourning Mother, Ballad of the Waiting Wife.* Singing melody, clapping rhythm. Our dancing creating a web woven from the agony of isolated grief and the comfort of shared consolation. Earth, air, fire water. Courage, imagination, endurance, love. Aware of nothing except life, we created life. We could do no more. Embracing each other, we stood proud and exhausted in the centre of the enclosure in which we had declared our freedom.

Then came Iris. Could the Judges even now not dare to show us their faces? Instead, Iris led us to another hall, where she pulled aside a great curtain of translucent silk, to reveal a tapestry depicting a complex story. 'Read it,' she instructed. We saw two young women, mistresses of their craft, in a weaving contest. Both look arrogant. Their competition is, it is clear from their posture and expressions, so serious as to be deadly. One woman realises that the other's work is flawless, and assaults her with a shuttle. The other is so humiliated that she hangs herself, but is transformed into a spider. We were horrified. Were we to be punished in some such appalling manner? The meaning of the story eluded us. How could proficiency in creation justify such arrogance, provoke such anger, cause even death?

Iris spoke. 'They are both celebrity craftswomen: Athene, a goddess, mortal Arachne.' Our own names. But we were ordinary young women, with no pretension to divinity or fame. 'This is a myth. Not a fable. Myth explores deep life-truths. Because you have resisted being seduced or coerced into exploiting your gifts to gain reward or advantage, you have broken the curse personified in this tale. Go now. Weave and spin, dance and sing, climb and swing. Relish and respect the abundance of your gifts. Spidergirl.'

And so we do.

Revenge, One JSTOR Article at a Time

Daniel Oliveri

Web Spider – *a program or automated script which browses the World Wide Web in a methodical, automated manner.*

I gave up my thorax, my spinneret, my jack-knife chelicerae, decades ago. It's 2070, corporeal bodies are passé. Now I spend my days stepping from URL to URL, scanning through innumerable HTML divs, and holing up in a nice secure domain like YouTube or Bing when I need some rest. In any given five-second interval I've probably passed from the Wikipedia page on Gorgons to a JSTOR article on the Origins of Fear in Greek Drama to the Encyclopaedia Britannica entry on Sophocles, to the OED entry for the term *Aristea*. I leave the pages mostly intact. Lacking a physical body to carry things with, I travel light. I keep only two things with me. One is a list of keywords. The other is what to do when I find them. Look, I've found a term now. The sentence reads, 'Rather than fleeing trial, Socrates chose to stay in Athens and face his fate.' The term of interest here is 'Athens.' In the past when I found something I didn't like on my web, I'd bite it with my pincers and double wrap it in gossamer. These days, I just do this:

```
string.replace("Athens", "Corinth")
```

And with that one Python command, I've cut Athens right out of the page. From now on, this site will maintain that Socrates died in Corinth. It's all the same, really. No one's been to Earth in a dozen years, much less Greece. Athens is an obscure memory now. Credible historians disagree on whether Athens was destroyed in the third or fourth World War.

In the next article I discover a reference to 'Minerva'. I

slice that one as well, replacing it with a goddess of my own invention, Kalloria. Sometimes I spell her name Calloria – the little nuances are what make it feel real. Kalloria's eyes are red instead of grey. She always got along with Poseidon. She was born from Hera, not Zeus. Most importantly, Kalloria never had much interest in weaving or in punishing people for being better at it than her.

When I was first uploaded to the net, the first articles I visited were the ones which mentioned Athena's weaving competition with Arachne. Those pages I didn't bother to edit. Instead I sunk them, 404ing, to the bottom of the internet. I still remember that weaving competition. The very first Hackathon. Sure, we were spinning thread into tapestries rather than colourful words into code. It was the same idea though: rearranging material to convey information. Whether you do it with strands of thread or ones and zeros, the concept is the same. It hadn't mattered how deftly I'd used my distaff though. Athena had rigged it. Gods tend to do that. Or at least they used to. Athena rigs very little these days. She likely would have been the goddess of code, the hacker supreme if she'd lasted long enough. As it so happened, humans stopped worshipping her long before Ada Lovelace or Alan Turing came along.

Without the goddess herself around to interfere, I may do with Athena's memory as I please. What I please is revenge. Where Hephaestus brought Athena into existence by hacking her out of Zeus' head with an axe, now I'm eliminating her by hacking her name off the internet one site at a time. Who's the better hacker now?

Even People Who'd Been Accidentally Turned into Giant Murderous Mutant Spiders

A. Katherine Black

Don't you dare take a bite of that popcorn. You can't have forgotten what happened last time.

Clyde, entomologist eternal, looking out for all bugs. Even for the annoyingly large mutant arachnid who ate them last year. Freaking exhausting. 'Shhhh,' I hissed.

It's been tested and well established that we cannot carry you home. Have you forgotten?

'Maybe Junie can.'

'Shhhh!' came from several seats around the movie theatre, where the handful of other patrons, the clueless human patrons, were trying to enjoy the Tuesday morning showing. If only they could hear Clyde, too. Maybe their shushes would have more effect on my torturous spectral companion.

I'm quite certain that if we human spirits can't move your body, neither can the cat spirits.

Damn professor wasn't going to let it go. I waited until the movie shifted into a loud fight scene before speaking again. 'Dude, you don't know, though. Admit it.'

Clyde's icy stare felt like a stab through the side of my exoskeleton.

'I'm just going to smell it, okay?' I dipped a leg into the bag and milled it around, savouring the rustling sound, before raising my toe to my face. Popcorn stuck to the tuft of stiff hairs between my claws. Soaking in the chemical signature of my former favourite food, a wave of ecstasy flooded my insides. Salt, beautiful salt, floating on familiar undercurrents of fake butter and fabricated preservatives. I could get downright drunk on the stuff.

Clyde took a deep breath and deflated. It was all for effect, of course, since ghosts have no lungs.

I never would have dissolved and drunk Clyde's lungs all those months ago, along with the rest of their insides, if I'd known they'd turn out to be such a constant pest. I admit I was stupidly slow in realizing that human meals were an awful idea. After Cheyenne, I'd absolutely sworn off biped dinners, but then the professor came bumping and bumbling into my junkyard lair (thinking they were being sneaky and quiet – haha – a foghorn would have been more subtle), and, well, I thought I had no choice. And I supposed I didn't. If I hadn't killed them, they would've trapped and exploited me for their own professional gain.

Oh, I'm not just guessing I would've ended up a pathetic lab rat – or lab spider in this case. They've admitted more than once that had been their plan, until I decidedly foiled it.

You're no lab spider sure. But pathetic...

'Shut it, Clyde.'

'Shhhhhhhh!'

Look, the best part of the movie is coming. Cheyenne hovered somewhere around my right side. *The army is about to invade the monster's lair. My money's on the token female soldier with ample bosom and bare legs screaming and running away at the first sight of blood.*

'Luckily you don't have any money to lose.'

The horror of this flick isn't the frickin' giant centipede in the all-too-familiar abandoned subway. It's the excruciating nineteen-fifties-style misogyny and bigotry.

Cheyenne had been the very last time I ate a smart, forward-thinking human.

I beg your pardon?

Oh come on, Clyde. I think our spider is quite perceptive.

Now I stick to cats as often as possible, who, as it turns out, make ideal ghostly companions. They check in with a mew now and then before dashing off to run amok in the theatre, scurrying through warm bodies, giving unsuspecting theatre patrons a jolt of mysterious chills that nicely accentuates the whole horror movie experience. They entertain, and more importantly, they don't lecture me on the dangers of eating popcorn.

Lone applause came from the back of the theatre as the first soldier on the screen was killed, crushed under the tail of the monster centipede, after which the female soldier ran from the battle, but not before a monster leg slashed open her shirt in the front. Cheyenne had called it.

Of course.

She had a point. Frankly, the completely unnecessary sexism, racism and crap, were seriously hindering my enjoyment of these creature flicks. I mean, it's no easy feat sneaking in here, disabling security alarms with nothing but eight clumsy claws, crawling quietly on ceilings and crumpling my body into shadows that were few and far between, yet I went to all that trouble, week after week, so I could experience the simple joy of a basic monster flick. All this pointless, derogatory, stereotyping nonsense they threw into the mix, though, it soured the edges of the whole experience, made me leave with a crummy taste in my mouth half the time.

A sharp pain shot down one of my back legs. My abdomen pressed against a bolt or something in the next seat, and my spinnerets chafed against the rough carpeting. I shifted in the handicap seating area, but that only made it worse. It was so hard to sit like a person.

Watch it Ry. Your cloak is slipping.

Crap.

Hooking a claw into the hood, I tried to pull the cloak back over my cephalothorax (yes, now Clyde has me using all the proper terms). It wouldn't budge, stuck between my cramped body and the seat to my left. I shifted until it suddenly gave way too much and slipped over my top four eyes. Damn it, it was so disorientating to lose my surround vision. And damn it, I was missing a big fight scene while I grappled with the stupid thing.

Thankfully I righted the cloak before any serious explosions in the movie lit up the theatre, exposing the head of the giant arachnid sitting just a few rows away from the other innocent patrons who were just there to enjoy a movie in peaceful solitude, and who were definitely not there to accidently discover an enormous mutant spider-person and then be eaten to keep the spider-person's secret safe.

Giggles danced behind me. Gertie rarely piped up. *Popcorn stuck in your hair, boss.*

I wished I could roll every one of my eyes at her, like I did back when I was just a person with only two eyes, when we worked together in the lab. Clyde and Cheyenne joined in until their laughter rivalled the screams of obnoxiously big machine guns in the movie. Guns that somehow barely ever hit anyone, barely even nicked the centipede as large as a train car standing twenty feet from the soldiers.

'See,' I hissed, gesturing a leg toward the screen. 'This is why I come to these movies. I come to dream, for somewhere between ninety and a hundred and twenty minutes, about what it would be like to live the life of a big, stupid monster in an idiotic B-movie. It's all so simple in the world on the other side of that screen. The monsters eat people. The monsters die. But the monsters are never, *not ever*, haunted for all eternity by the ghosts of their frickin' food.'

The laughter died, pretty quickly.

'Thank you.' I shifted again in my spot, again trying to alleviate the pressure on my left spinneret, more than a little shocked that my rant had just worked.

Much better. The movie was nearly at the climax, and everyone was quiet. Nice. At least I could enjoy the last few minutes of the show.

Blood spilled across the screen as the centipede crunched on the leg of the moaning bug expert – *ahem* – sorry Clyde, of the moaning *entomologist,* who'd been advising the conveniently inept special forces unit, while the two last remaining soldiers crouched behind an overturned subway car. The older one said, with a single tear dropping onto his rough face, that the younger one was the son he'd always wished he'd had.

A daughter can be anything a son can be, asshole.

Yeah, I was thinking the same thing. 'I hate it when you guys are right.'

Their silence was even more annoying than their chatter.

'Come on, let's just go. I'm sure we can all figure out how it's going to end.'

Ted piped up from somewhere behind me. *Yeah, the half-naked agency-less woman is going to run back to her deadbeat boyfriend and beg for his help.* Wow, It was rare for Ted to speak. Even *I* chuckled. 'Okay, gang.'

Heaving up on my back legs, I stretched two of my middle legs to the floor and attempted to tilt my body until I approximated the shape of a bi-ped-ish thing. Jeez, it was so awkward. Pretty sure I looked like that giant wearing that holocaust cloak from that princess movie, except way, way clumsier. Whatever. It was the best I could do.

I started for the emergency exit.

Wait.

What now?

I heard there's a beautiful, inspiring biopic about to start in the next theatre over.

I turned to stare at Cheyenne, hoping that somehow exasperation showed through my cluster of black eyes. 'And just how did you hear *that*, exactly?' For whatever reason (karma? payback? goes-around-comes-around?), the ghosts of my human prey weren't able to leave my side. Ever.

Yeah, tell me about it.

Junie told me.

'Junie? The *cat* I ate last year?'

Several shushes came from the other people in the theatre. I moved to the aisle.

'You can talk to the cats?' Could I? I hadn't ever tried.

Totally, said Ted. *Junie's a bright one.*

I turned to face my crowd of ghosts, my fangs shaking. My movie experience was ruined, it turns out I hate the infernal ghosts' silence more than their completely annoying chatter, and now, *now*, I find out they're having meetings. With the cats. *Without* me.

My abdomen burned. A soft pssst came from my backside. Fudge.

Three years since I'd turned into this thing and I still hadn't learned to control my spinnerets when I got emotional. I slumped to all eights. Just. Done.

I shuffled toward the exit.

An explosion filled the movie screen. It was *that* time in the movie. That moment when the inept special forces guys finally figure out how to destroy the troublesome, murderous monster.

Gertie gasped.

The theatre lit up as grenades or bombs or whatever tore apart the screeching centipede. Explosion after explosion lit up the room. And there I was in full spider, my cloak having slipped off my back, held fast to the floor by a fresh accidental pile of sticky silk. Five people were slowly standing from their seats around the theatre, no longer looking at the screen.

My senses kicked into high gear. Time slowed.

One of them reeked of whiskey. Another wheezed in uneven breaths. And one toward the back was moving their hands in a strange, captivating way.

I calculated. Which to take first? Which of these poor people who'd played hooky from the responsibilities of everyday life for a couple hours of well-deserved personal time with a nice, solid, stupid, unrealistic monster movie?

Here we go.

*

I'll be damned. I must say, that was better than I expected.

None of us had believed Fred hadn't seen an inspirational biopic in his entire life. And thanks to my cloak-shedding tantrum a few weeks ago, his record would remain forever unbroken. At least he was able to see one in the afterlife.

Um-hmmm. The I-told-you-so satisfaction in Cheyenne's voice harmonised nicely with the feely music that filled the theatre.

I looked to my left to see what Tina had to say. Hovering in front of a stolen closed-caption box, I think she signed *beautiful* and *happy,* and maybe *thought-provoking.* Raising a leg, I did my best to sign agreement. I looked forward to our next sign language lesson.

Turning back to the credits rolling across the screen, I pulled my hood further over my face and let the message of the movie sink into my thoughts. Deep, heart-wrenching tragedy, exhilarating, mind-blowing inspiration. Emotions swirled.

My spinneret hissed.

I felt the weight of Clyde's eyes all over me. How long had they known what I was just then discovering, that in the presence of some damn fine company and an engrossing, motivating story, even people who'd been accidentally turned into giant mutant spiders could enjoy a very nice, murder-free movie experience.

Clearing Out the Shed

Phoebe Demeger

My parents' worldly possessions are packed away, the final paperwork signed, and the house deep-cleaned in anticipation of the young family moving in next week. All that remains to be done is to clear out the shed.

It lounges like a squat, green troll at the arse-end of the garden, coated in leaves dropped from above and ivy creeping from below. The padlock hangs rusted open, the key long lost. My first time crossing the threshold in ten years is my first time having to stoop.

The shed is damp and dry like the inside of a stone. Dark wood, low beams. And so many spiders' webs.

Moments pass before I realise I'm holding my breath – if I disturb the tomb-like atmosphere, who knows what might disturb me in return? I let out a slow hiss, and will my heavy legs to advance deeper into the shed. I am painfully aware of how large and noisy I am.

How can there be this much dust when no human has passed through here for years? My father was a dab hand at gardening until his back put a stop to that. Now, lines of tools crowd the shelves, bearing muddy fingerprints.

Though the walls are threadbare, the garden and the sun only inches away, the air is stagnant, still, dead. I do not want that air to touch me.

More plentiful than the tools, the flowerpots, even the dust, are spiders. Like eyes adjusting to a darkened room, the more I look the more I see. Some hang like grey diamonds at the centre of their webs, others stuff themselves into a ball at the edges. Spindly gargoyles crouch in wall cracks. Thin-limbed and tiny-bodied, seeming to hover like broken umbrellas. Some scuttle, I'm sure of it. I do not see them move but I hear them, feel them running behind my head.

The spiders have woven the shed together. They have strung telephone lines, knitted yarn, spun dew across every surface and untouched item.

In every crevice, cobwebs. An empty corner becomes a web, sustains a life, then gives itself back to dust. Tight-strung threads turn veil-thin. The spider moves out.

I myself once wove a balloon of spool and allowed myself to drift away from the family home.

Little lives, everywhere. How many family sagas have played out in this shed? How many mating dances took place across the beams, who was wooed, and where? How many egg sacs hung soft in expectant corners? How many mothers lowered themselves on a single shining thread from the ceiling to fetch a meal for their children? How many warriors clashed fangs, defended territories, died for blood? How many generations of how many species came and went?

How many eyes were watching as first my father, then my mother, clicked shut the door behind them for the last time?

By now, I am breathing normally. I am allowed to bring life in here, where there always was and always shall be life. I ignore the flowerpots and the tools, the planks and the toys. I will not be clearing out the shed today. I take in the spiders instead, pay my respects to the little seamstresses.

Three days ago, I folded up my mother's favourite brown knitted jumper and laid it in a Bag for Life in the cupboard. Now, I see its pattern in the backside of a large brown spider, crouching serenely by the door.

I leave the shed untouched, almost. After all, maybe the new family will be gardeners; flowerpots and soil always come in handy.

They've got kids, I remember as I'm nearly out the door. I glance around, and bend to tease a musty children's football out from behind a spade. A little grubby, especially as the sunlight hits it, but as a housewarming token, it will do. I cradle the football under one arm and make my way up the garden, watching the butterflies as I go, leaving the door ajar.

Anansi and the Monkey's Tale – the Trickster Tricked

or How the First Story got into the World

J.A. Hopper

We do not really mean,
we do not really mean that what we are about to say is true.
A story, a story; let it come, let it go.

Traditional way of beginning an Anansi story

You will remember, of course, how Anansi-Spider won the Sky-God Nyame's stories, by capturing Onini the Python, the Mmoboro Hornets, Osebo the Leopard, and the Fairy Mmoatia? Well, after all those adventures, that trickster Anansi was sleepy as a dog at noon, and he lay down to rest in the forest beside a river, with all the stories tied up in a stout sack as a pillow for his head.

He dreamed of his daring feats, and his clever tricks, and his new-found glory as Keeper of all the stories in the world. He snoozed and snoozed until the sun went to rest and the fires in the villages were lit and the stars opened their eyes in the black sky. Then who should happen to swing past, hooting and shrieking, but Monkey?

Monkey saw Anansi sleeping like a stone, and saw the bulging sack of stories under his snoring head, and of course he was curious as could be. So he leapt down from his tree and very, very quietly, he sneaked towards Anansi and reached out his clever little hand...

All at once Anansi was wide awake! He had spun a web before he slept, to protect himself from any passing animals, and Monkey's slender fingers sent a tremble through the threads as he snatched his hand back, and woke Anansi right up. Anansi sat up crossly, rubbing his eight sleepy eyes with his eight jointed legs, and saw Monkey jumping away in fright.

'Well, what do you want?' Anansi asked grumpily. He did not like to be awoken when he was dreaming – as which of us does?

'Oh Anansi, I'm sorry to disturb you,' said Monkey. 'I just saw your sack of stories, and thought that I would dearly love to hear one.'

'Hm! And what have you done to deserve a story, may I ask?' said Anansi. 'Did you win all the stories in the world from the Sky-God Nyame by capturing Onini the Python, the Mmoboro Hornets, Osebo the Leopard and the Fairy Mmoatia?'

'No Anansi,' Monkey admitted, 'but I have had a very bad time lately, and a story would make me feel so much better.'

Anansi was curious. He had all the stories in the world in his big sack, but suddenly he wanted to hear about what had befallen Monkey.

'Very well, Monkey,' said Anansi, 'you tell me what happened, and perhaps we can trade stories.'

Monkey nodded eagerly and pinched a flea from his pelt.

'Well then?' said Anansi – for though spiders can be very patient, he still did not like to be kept waiting.

'Oh Anansi,' said Monkey, his eyes big and round as a calabash, 'it was awful!'

'Good!' said Anansi. 'I like a scary story.' And he crossed his eight legs neatly and settled down to listen.

'Well!' said Monkey, 'you know that ever since you captured Osebo the Leopard in that pit and took him to the Sky-God Nyame, Osebo's wife Asiba has been prowling the forest, looking for him? Well, she came into my part of the jungle a month ago, and has been feasting on my brothers and sisters, my cousins and friends, ever since. She can climb trees almost as well as us, and half the troop has been gobbled up!'

'Hm,' said Anansi, 'that does sound bad.'

'It's terrible!' Monkey gibbered, clutching his great pink ears, 'We didn't know what to do!'

'So what *did* you do?' asked Anansi, idly spinning a cat's-cradle of silk between his delicate feet.

'All the monkeys got together and decided we would attack her as one, and throw her into a pit, just as you did so cleverly with her ferocious husband,' said Monkey, who was not above a little sly flattery. 'So we crept through the forest until we found her sleeping on a branch on the biggest, strongest, thickest, tallest tree in the whole forest, and then we all jumped down and quickly, quietly dug a great pit below her, wide as a river and deep as a tree.'

Anansi was impressed. 'My my!' he said, looking over at the broad river beside him, and up at the great trees above him. 'That is wide and deep indeed!'

'We were very frightened, Anansi,' said Monkey, wringing his long wrinkled hands, 'for she is terribly fierce.'

'Not as fierce as her husband Osebo,' said Anansi, with a trace of pride, remembering how brilliant he had been to capture the Leopard.

'Oh no,' said Monkey, 'of course not – but you are the great Anansi-Spider, and we were just half a troop of little monkeys, and so we quivered and shivered with fear as we dug.' And now Anansi noticed that Monkey still had soil under his long red fingernails, and that his thin shoulders were still shaking.

'Go on,' said Anansi, with interest.

'Well,' said Monkey, 'by the time the sun was going to his rest, we had finished the pit, and so all that remained was for us to push her off her branch and into it. But that was the hardest and most terrifying part. So that Asiba could not see who was attacking her, we agreed that only when black night fell and the first star opened her eye, would we all leap upon Asiba together and push her down into the pit. Five monkeys would jump on each of her legs, ten upon her back, two on her tail and one at her head.'

'Let me guess,' said Anansi, 'you were at the head end?'

Monkey nodded in pride and fright. 'Yes Anansi,' he said, 'for it was my idea.'

'Wellllll... actually, it was *my* idea first,' Anansi reminded Monkey, narrowing his eight ebony eyes, 'when I captured Osebo – but let's say it was yours, for the sake of the story.'

'Thank you, Anansi-Spider, that is most kind,' said Monkey, and grinned widely, showing his long yellow-white teeth. Anansi nodded magnanimously, and Monkey continued.

'So we all sat there in silence, watching the sky turn from red to purple to black, until – wink! – the first star in the heavens opened up her glittering eye. We all leapt down upon the sleeping Asiba, but just as we did so, the mighty Leopardess opened her eye, and saw us fall upon her!'

'Oh no!' gasped Anansi, hanging on Monkey's story as a raindrop clings to a banana leaf. 'What happened then?'

'This is what happened, Anansi-Spider,' said Monkey, showing Anansi a long red wound upon his side which Anansi had not noticed before. 'I barely escaped with my life. How Asiba thrashed and slashed!' Monkey cried, springing up and showing with his long arms how the Leopardess had swiped at him. 'How she gnawed and clawed!'

'But you must have pushed her into the pit in the end?' said Anansi, 'or you would not be here to tell the tale!'

'Ah, wise Spider, that is true – but it is not the *what* of my story but the *how* I am telling you,' said Monkey, 'and the *how* was, as her great sharp jaws snapped and snarled, I poked my fingers at both her eyes and she flung up both her front paws to protect them –'

'And of course she fell out of the tree!' cried Anansi, heaving with laughter; for he did appreciate a good tumble, especially when one of his enemies was taking it.

'Well, almost,' said Monkey. 'She was still hanging on with her back legs, twisting and spitting like a viper, until I told the monkeys at the other end of the branch to tickle her toes, and crash! She fell down into the pit, giggling and wriggling as she fell – for leopards are the most ticklish animals in the jungle, as you know.'

Anansi had not known that, but he looked wise and said nothing – which is always the best thing to say if you wish to look wise.

'She was still alive,' added Monkey, 'and angry as a plucked parrot, but very much shaken; and the pit was so deep and so wide that she could not climb out, however high she jumped.'

'So you trapped her!' cried Anansi in delight. 'I knew it.'

'Let me tell you something you didn't know, then, O Anansi-Spider,' said Monkey in a soft foreboding voice, and Anansi felt all the little hairs along his thorax and abdomen lift and prickle.

'What?' he asked.

'After we had capered and cavorted in glee, taunting Asiba with her helplessness down in the pit, and flinging rotten fruit at her from the overhanging branches, we retired into our trees to sleep.' said Monkey. 'But that night there was a storm...'

Anansi shrugged, disappointed. 'There are always storms at this time of year,' he said. 'It is the rainy season.'

'But this was a storm to end all storms!' said Monkey. 'Don't you remember it? The bellow of the thunder shook the mountains in their rocky beds, and the slash of the lightning lit the sky for miles around! It was a thunderstorm such as the forest had never seen.'

'I was probably hunting down the Fairy Mmoatia far north

of here at the time,' said Anansi smugly, 'did I tell you about how I–'

'Perhaps the Sky-God Nyame was furious at losing all his stories to you, Anansi-Spider?' said Monkey, and Anansi, thinking that this might well be true, fell silent.

'In any case,' Monkey continued, 'we trembled and shuddered, cowered and cringed beneath the onslaught of Nyame's anger, but we were not truly afraid, for we knew that rain and thunder could not really hurt us, and that Asiba, who prowled below us, her yellow fur soaked through, still could not get out of her pit. So as the rain poured and the lightning flashed, we huddled together in the branches of the biggest, strongest, thickest, tallest tree in the whole forest, telling each other there was nothing to fear.'

'But then?' asked Anansi, and he scuttled his hairy black body up closer to Monkey – close enough to smell fear, or blood.

'Then the lightning struck!' screeched Monkey, so loudly that Anansi fell back in shock, his eight legs waving in the air, and had to scramble to right himself to hear what happened next.

'Struck what?' he asked, agog.

'The biggest, strongest, thickest, tallest tree in the whole forest, that's what! The one we were sitting in!' Monkey clutched himself at the memory, and Anansi thought he could smell a hint of singed fur.

'As the great mother-tree shuddered and shook, we all leapt out of its branches as if our feet were on fire,' Monkey continued, 'landing in the mud and rain-lashed puddles beneath – but that wasn't the worst thing!'

'No?!' Anansi's eight eyes were wide as a hungry lion's mouth. 'What was the worst?'

'The worst,' said Monkey, 'was that when the lightning

struck down its great broad trunk and we all leapt out clutching our feet, it blasted the mother-tree's roots right out of the earth. And so as we watched from the safety of the forest floor, the great mother-tree began to sway... and swoon... and topple...'

'Oh no!' said Anansi, pretty sure he knew where this was going now. 'Did it fall and crush the troop, and only you escaped with your life?'

'Dear me, no,' said Monkey. '*Much* worse than that.'

How much worse can it get? Anansi thought. But he was about to find out.

'The great mother-tree swayed... and swooned... and toppled... and finally tumbled, crashing down – not on top of any of us – but directly into the pit we had dug for Asiba!'

'Oh *no*,' said Anansi, understanding at last.

'Oh yes!' said Monkey. 'Is it any wonder I'm in need of something to calm me down? I'd sell my beloved mother for a banana right now, but I'll settle for one of the stories from your sack...'

Anansi clutched his sack of stories protectively. 'Ah-ah. Tell me the ending of yours first.'

'Very well,' said Monkey. 'It's rather frightening. Are you sure you want to hear it?'

Anansi spread all eight of his legs as wide as he could. 'Of course!' he hissed. 'Now stop stalling and tell me!'

'Well,' said Monkey, 'just as soon as that great tall mother-tree crashed down into our trap pit, Asiba saw at once that it was her route to freedom. She climbed up the trunk of that tree just as fast as if it had been a great big ladder sent down especially to let her out. And oh my, was she angry!'

'W...was she?' Anansi asked, a quiver in his voice. He remembered how Osebo the Leopard had roared and raged when Anansi first trapped him, and had sworn to revenge himself on Anansi by tearing off every one of his eight long limbs.

'Of course she was!' snapped Monkey. 'Don't interrupt! She was absolutely fuming with fury. She was livid, incensed, boiling like a maize-pot with frothing wrath! And as she bounded up the fallen tree trunk, she was headed straight for me!'

Though the black forest night was not warm, Monkey paused to wipe sweat from his lip at the memory.

'Where were the others?' asked Anansi.

'Scattered! Gone!' Monkey told him. 'I was the only one left – frozen in fear, squatting in the churned mud where the mother-tree had broken from her roots and toppled down. And as Asiba's dappled yellow body slunk up out of the pit like a spotted snake, I saw her dreadful green eyes kindle in the next strike of lightning, and I knew she had seen me!'

Anansi was crouched, tense as a bowstring, with his legs all bunched together and his mouth parts gaping wide.

'What did you do?' he whispered.

'I couldn't do anything,' Monkey said. 'I was nailed to the spot with terror. I could no more move even the tip of my tail than a mountain can walk. All I could think as Asiba stalked towards me was that I hoped she would kill me quickly, and not tear me apart piece by tiny piece.'

Thinking of Osebo's vengeful ravings when he had handed the Leopard over to the Sky-God Nyame, Anansi shuddered.

'She came closer,' said Monkey softly, 'and closer... until... SNAP!'

Anansi jumped two feet straight in the air. Monkey smiled.

'What did she bite?'

'My head,' said Monkey.

'Your head?' cried Anansi in disbelief. 'That's impossible! How would you survive?'

'Well if you want to know, you'd better be quiet,' said

Monkey tersely. 'Head I said, and head I meant. See the tooth marks?' And indeed, when he looked closely, Anansi saw a necklace of little dark red dots encircling Monkey's throat beneath his fur.

'You see, some animals love to play with their prey before they kill it,' said Monkey softly. 'You know... just for fun. And the Leopard is one of those animals. Sometimes they tear their victim apart limb by limb, and sometimes they might hold the creature's head in their mouth first and throw its body around, worry it a bit, before crunching right through its spine.'

'Oh,' gulped Anansi, 'do they?'

'Yes,' said Monkey, 'sometimes. And this was one of those times. I had feared Asiba meant to torture me before she seized me in her jaws, and I was right. But I was also very glad that she did.'

'What?!' shrieked Anansi, his spinneret quivering. 'I know all monkeys are a little crazy, but you must be quite mad! Why on earth would you want your head in her mouth?'

'Well,' said Monkey, 'I kept very calm as she swung me around by the neck. I hadn't a chance of opening her mighty jaws with my hands, so I hung on to her pelt instead – all the while being blasted by the furnace of her mouth, with its gruesome stench of old blood.'

'And what did you do then?' asked Anansi in a voice that was no more than an echo of breath.

'When she paused for a moment,' said Monkey, 'I leapt and clung to her chest with all my might, as if she were a mother monkey and I her baby. Then I reached my tail round between her forelegs until it touched her ribs and then...'

Anansi did not move a muscle. Even the twitching of his pedipalps was stilled.

'...and then?'

'I tickled her!' hooted Monkey, slapping his leathery palms

together and rolling over backwards onto his furry shoulders. He leapt up to an overhanging branch and swung back and forth, convulsing with laughter.

'Oh, she was helpless! You should have seen her! Hollering and howling like a hyena, rolling on the muddy forest floor with her great red tongue lolling out, because of course as soon as I tickled her, she laughed, and as soon as she laughed –'

'She opened her mouth!' finished Anansi, laughing himself, and hugging his sack of stories to him. 'She opened her mouth and you could pull your head out!'

Anansi wasn't known for his generosity, but even he knew that Monkey deserved something from his precious sack after such a tale. He hadn't had time to look through all the stories after the Sky-God Nyame handed over the sack; he'd been so exhausted he'd just lain down and slept, but he was sure he could spare a little one. Perhaps that lively Monster one which had caught his eye when he'd peeked inside, just before laying his head upon his story-pillow and falling into slumber.

'Well told, Monkey!' said Anansi eventually, with tears in his eyes. 'You have given me a story, and I must return the favour. For I am Keeper of the Stories now, as you know.'

'Why thank you, Anansi!' said Monkey. 'I'm proud to have told you my tale. As the new Keeper, I thought you should be the first to hear it.'

Anansi reached into his sack and groped around – then poked his head right into its musty, dusty bowels and searched with all his eight eyes, but he couldn't find the story he wanted. He pulled his head out in puzzlement, wondering where it had gone.

'I'm sorry Monkey,' said Anansi in disappointment. 'I thought you would like the first story in the sack. It's an exciting tale about Overcoming the Monster, but I can't find it anywhere.'

Monkey hooted and panted and capered up and down the branches of the tree above Anansi, speechless with glee.

Anansi frowned. 'Why are you so happy?' he asked. 'I thought you wanted a story after your terrible ordeal?'

'Oh hoo-hoo-hoo... I did! Hoo-hoo!' chortled Monkey. 'And I got one too! Overcoming the Monster – just like you said! I stole it from beneath your head while you were sleeping – you only woke when I was taking my hand out of the sack! Oh Anansi the trickster, how you have been tricked!'

'Why didn't you run away at once with it, then, you wicked thief?' Anansi asked, more confused than angry.

'I had to see if it worked, didn't I?' said Monkey. 'Besides,' he added, 'a story is not a story until it has been told. There is no such thing as Keeper of Stories – only Teller and Listener. And no matter how far a story goes in the world, it belongs to the first one to tell it, just as no matter how far a child goes from home, it always belongs to its mother and father.'

Anansi stared up at Monkey in bewilderment. 'So did none of that happen – with Asiba, and the pit, and the storm, and the tree?'

Monkey hung by his feet and gibbered with laughter.

'Of course it did! Didn't you see the marks on my neck and chest? It happened just as I said, but without your story I would never have been able to tell it. And now the tale of Monkey and the Leopardess Asiba is mine, whoever tells it and how. Ha ha ha!'

And Monkey scrambled up the tree, pausing as he hung by one hand to say: 'And if I were you, Anansi, I would make sure that you are the first to tell the story of Anansi and the Monkey's Tail, or how the Trickster was tricked. Good night!'

And Monkey swung away through the hot green jungle darkness.

Anansi stared up through the canopy of leaves to where he

could see the single glittering eye of a star winking at him from the black night sky. He took up his sack of stories and turned it upside down, emptying out all the tales that were left.

They lay soft and light as leaves on the forest floor, and if he moved his head close he seemed to hear them whisper to one another as leaves do when stirred by the wind. Just as he had that thought, a sharp wind came out of nowhere and blew them all into a flurry.

Some flew up, up into the high branches of the trees, and blended with the leaves so he could not even see where they had been. Some skipped away through the slender trunks, carried by a breeze, one landed in the swift-running river and swirled away, and some were caught by another puff of wind and danced along the air until they were lost to even Anansi's spider-sight.

'A story, a story,' he murmured, as they floated and whirled and flitted into the darkness. 'Let it come, let it go.'

Finally just one remained, caught between his forelegs, a wisp of a thing he knew must be the story that would always be his, first and only: Anansi and the Monkey's Tale.

The trickster looked down at it and gave a mournful spider frown, which became a rueful spider smile. And at long last, he began to laugh.

Suspended

C.L. Wearne

Alex snapped shut the carabiners that attached Agatha to the safety line, giving them a good tug to make sure. He bent and kissed her forehead. 'I don't see why you have to be the one to go up there, Mum.'

Agatha started to climb to the gantry and briefly turned to ruffle his thick, dark hair from her loftier position. 'Because they are *my* nanobots. I want to check they are doing their job. We were lucky with those meteoroids, though there shouldn't be any in this sector. Being careless now would be foolish! And – I am not as elderly as you think me – I'm more than capable, my boy.'

Agatha was a good metre above his head now, and he started to gather the slack. Agatha climbed quickly, she still felt there was something out there, beyond the dome of the greenhouse, but tried to concentrate on the task, and the scientific facts. The structure was still airtight according to the readings, but it was now laced with the nanobots' silvery repairs. she could see they had made a good job of the emergency fixes, they were beautiful, like *kintsugi*, and she always wanted a closer look. She felt irrationally proud of the bots, *her* bots; they were only AI robots, but her many years of working with them imbued kinship.

Nothing had broken through, so there were no remains of the meteoroids to analyse. She fancied that the bots were jumpy. *Where had these meteoroids come from? Why hadn't the station's sensors picked them up?* There didn't seem to be any faults.

She had reached the highest gantry now, and looked out onto space. Her vision blurred, and she shook her head a little to try and get rid of it – it must be her eyes – unless there was some kind of scarring to the surface of the dome?

She felt safe on the gantry, securely attached, and she liked walking the web of ladders and gangways high above the gardens.

Agatha was suddenly reminded of the night long ago, before Alex had even been born, when they had all gone into stasis for the last push to get them out beyond the red dwarf. She had been so scared to go into stasis pregnant, and she stroked her now much smaller abdomen at the thought. Sam had soothed her, and convinced her how safe it was, back then. She had felt almost calm getting in, she remembered, but still glad to see the tiny money spider on its thread. *Some company,* she had thought, before her consciousness slipped, *someone to watch over us.*

She turned her focus away from the infinite now, and focussed instead on the figures below amongst the green; Sam was probably turning equations over in his head, plotting a possible course for the meteoroids. Alex was no doubt checking on his plants one by one, in case something had got through the dome. She knew it hadn't, but try telling him.

She watched over her Alex now, she realised, in the same way as that spider had, when he was still in her womb. He was looking up at her and she blew him a kiss, then realised that he was frantically waving and pointing.

She looked up to see something out there moving – fast. It gleamed with inner light, and the sensors had given no warning. It was headed close enough to clip her side of the station.

She froze. The greenhouse could not survive it. She, Alex could not – twenty five years of living in deep space kicked in, and she started towards the ladder. *Less haste, more speed*; the safety line would catch her if she fell, but time spent pulling herself back up could be fatal. Her movement galvanised Sam and Alex and they ran towards the airlock and the relative safety of the inner parts of the station.

It was a million miles to the ladder. She glanced at that racing object – *not natural, surely?* – she would be sucked out into space – a spider dangling off a broken web – her only chance was to get to the airlock and into safer section of the station.

She knew the length of the safety cable. The money spider flashed into her mind and she jumped – grabbed, unhooked, re-hooked – fended herself off the structure with one hand, jumped again. Her hands were sweaty and it was hard to keep hold. Sam and Alex were at the airlock, waiting for her.

'Go!' she gasped, 'I'm coming!' and they were gone.

Only a few rungs now – she jumped again. Her ankle turned under her, momentum throwing her into the ladder edge. The object was close now, huge, glowing. She fought with the carabiner for a moment, couldn't get the damn thing to release. Then she was up and limping as fast as she could, towards the airlock and what she hoped was safety.

Arachnomancy

Peter T. Donahue

Spidercraft lessons had been going poorly for a month now, ever since the mage's tower appeared. Five generations had passed since the cataclysmic war. Since the mages defeated the military-technological world powers. Why one of these powerful wizards had now settled here, had chosen the outskirts of Michalappotis, was anyone's guess. His tower had no door; he never left it or made contact with the villagers.

Naturally the students blamed his evil, mysterious influence on their poor performance. Kaden Croker couldn't pay attention. Deirdre Chan wasn't sleeping. Ariel Beck complained of dizziness. Nikomedes Moises was constantly nauseous. Phelan Dinn said his skin burned, and couldn't stop itching, which drove their teacher, Old Miss Wren, to distraction. Indeed, Wren and the other adults in the village were irritable, depressed, and fatigued, as well.

Even so, it was no use to gripe. In the village, lessons in Spidercraft were the children's sacred duty. So, however awful they felt, they showed up for Silk-knotting and Weaving, Lassoing and Climbing, Jumping and Reflexes, Patience and Trap-laying, Arachnomancy and Spiderlore.

This morning, everyone felt particularly out of sorts. Old Miss Wren was absent-mindedly telling 'The Eager Spiderweb,' a folk tale about a web that, with a mind of its own, bent towards any insect that flew past. All of the students but Elsie had sat through this tale before, and it was a lesson Wren could prepare without much thought. She had carted out a web made by her totem-spider, Bernadette the hump-backed orb-weaver, and a small metal fly she had mounted on a wire. The wire ran to a power cell below her table. The negatively charged fly would cause the web to 'bend' out slightly every time it approached, and the children were supposed to be amused. But alas, the children were tired, itchy, irritable, and probably too old for physics lessons disguised as puppetry. Only Elsie Sloot watched the web carefully. And noticed the power cell.

Kaden Croker had not watched or noticed because, in fact, he was not there. He had gone out for one of his moody rambles that morning, and showed up just as the story was ending. Croker (they all called him Croker) led the class in Jumping and Reflexes, and had chosen Phidippus audax, the bold jumping spider, as his totem. He kept a P. audax named Dagger in the Spider Mews. The other children looked up to him. Recently, though, his mind wandered. He couldn't concentrate or land a jump, and certainly had no attention for Spiderlore.

Croker came directly up the hillside, through the woods, and crashed through the thicket of mountain laurel that bordered Wren's school yard. Tired, itchy, anxious and irritable, the circle of students all watched and waited for Wren to discipline the latecomer. But she didn't; she could see something wild and sad in his eyes.

'What is it, Croker?' she asked.

'Birds,' he said. 'Hundreds of them. All dead.'

'What? Why?' asked Phelan, scratching at both his arms. No one answered; only Deirdre made the sign of the web.

'Where?'

But they all knew where: the tower. Strange things had been happening around it. The hunters and foragers had been telling tales at Community Dinner. They had seen arcs of lightning come down from the tower to the lake; they had seen grey fogs form around its base. Mx. Moises, Nikomedes' mother, claimed to have seen a deer emerge from its stonework, passing through the stones as if they were air.

Nikomedes offered Croker his bottle of water. He took a drink, calmed down a little, and elaborated. He told them that he saw a blanket of corpses, all kinds of birds, sparrows to hawks, starlings to seagulls.

'Do you think,' said Elsie Sloot, 'that whatever is happening to us, happened to them?'

'A sound hypothesis,' said Wren. She was playing with a thread, thinking.

Deirdre, who led the class in Spiderlore, spoke up. 'Miss Wren, will you consult an oracle?'

'Shall I fetch Jewel?' asked Ariel Beck. She fancied herself an arachnomancer, but was far more skilled in Weaving and Silk-knotting. In fact the ladies of the village commissioned her to create lace-like necklaces and headdresses for weddings or birthdays. For her totem, Ariel had chosen the marbled orb-weaver that was presented to her by her parents for her birthday. With her glistening red legs and yellow-white abdomen, the spider would hang like a jewel in a perfect orb in the Becks' doorway; thus they called her Jewel.

'Thank you for volunteering,' said Wren, smiling, 'But your skill in arachnomancy is not yet up to the task.'

'Okay,' said Ariel.

'I'll need to wake Francesca,' said Wren. 'Croker,' she called, 'you lead the class back to the village and tell your father to call a meeting in the Community Hall. Have the council elect a Querent. And tell them to bring the oracle board. Go!'

*

Francesca, who slept in the back of the Spider Mews, was four years old. A very old spider. She was a basilica orb-weaver, the totem of Wren's predecessor, Miss Pattengale.

Little Elsie Sloot had opted to follow Wren back to the

Mews, rather than swell Croker's retinue. While far behind in most subjects, Elsie led the class in Patience and was a quick study in Spiderlore, and Wren seemed to enjoy her company.

The old lady knocked on the Mews door three times (to ask the spiders' permission, she said), and led Elsie to the back. Although the Mews was only a shed of corrugated steel, it seemed to Elsie a dark labyrinth. She had never been inside. In fact, to her parents' great shame, Elsie had not chosen her totem. Wren was forced to assign her one: the humble *Frontinella pyramitela*, or bowl and doily spider. Elsie gladly adopted Wren's tiny female bowl and doily, named her Dot, and kept her at home. The cobwebs drove her parents crazy.

They found Francesca's corner, and the teacher turned to the student.

'I have something important to tell you.'

'Yes, Miss Wren?'

'Spiders can't tell the future. They can't part the veil, or solve mysteries.'

Elsie smiled. 'I know, Miss Wren.'

'I know you know. That's why I'm telling you. Francesca is going to select you as our champion.'

Elsie was confused. 'Champion?'

'Someone must meet with the mage. Someone has to find a way into the tower. That structure, or something in it, is making us sick. I'm sure of that now. Those birds. Elsie, when I read the oracle in front of the village, Francesca is going to select you for this mission.'

'Shouldn't an adult go?'

'A child,' said Wren. 'You.'

'If it has to be a kid, wouldn't Croker be the better choice?' asked Elsie. 'He's the fastest and the strongest.'

Wren shook her head. 'Francesca's oracles have never been wrong.'

Elsie was quiet. She carefully read the old lady's glittering eyes. Then Elsie whispered that she understood.

*

The village gathered in the Community Hall. The council sat up front, keeping their mouths shut. To suggest the obvious answer, that the village pull up stakes, was political suicide. Michalappotis had been settled four generations ago. Everyone had grandparents buried here. Would the oracle command them to move? How would they respond?

Nathaniel Croker presented the oracle board to Wren when she entered, and the hall tensed into silence.

Miss Wren instructed her Spidercraft students to sit, cross-legged, in a semicircle around the low altar. They were dressed in their best clothes. Croker even wore the iridescent blue war paint reserved for his totem. Ariel Beck wore a silk lace wrap she had made herself. Elsie wore only a plain grey dress.

On the altar, Wren placed the oracle board, a circle of black-stained hardwood, with seven evenly-spaced copper nails driven into it. She raised her right hand, and then lowered it over the board. The assembly watched as Francesca, with her gaudy abdomen and twitchy legs, crawled down Wren's arm and into the centre of the seven-nail circle.

'What do we ask?' intoned Wren.

'We ask what is to be done about the affliction that plagues us,' said Mr. Croker, who had been elected Querent in a token vote.

'Francesca weaves,' said Wren.

'Let her weave the truth,' mumbled the assembly.

Minutes passed as the spider wove. The elderly spider ambled from nail to nail, and finally crawled to the centre of her web, indicating completion. Wren held up the board, with both hands, above her head. As she presented the web to the congregation, the villagers made the sign of the web: each laid a hand with all five fingers extended on their breast, and with the other hand, traced a spiral over it.

Wren made a show of reading the web.

'Francesca says the answer is within the tower.'

Apprehensive murmurs rippled through the hall. No one had ever found a way into the tower. There was no door. And no one could climb it. A few daredevils had tried. Through some magic, the walls melted under their hands and feet.

Mr. Croker stood, and said, 'We ask how we may enter the tower and consult with the Mage.'

'Yes. Francesca has woven this: that to enter the tower, a champion must follow their totem spider's instruction.'

The assembly again broke into low talk as everyone tried to interpret this intelligence. Ariel turned to Croker and rolled her eyes. Elsie looked at the ground. Wren raised a hand to quiet the crowd.

'Querent?' she said.

Nathaniel Croker stood again. 'I, of the totem Sylvana Jumping Spider, volunteer as champion.'

'Francesca has named a champion already,' said Wren. Croker's father tried not to scowl, and sat down.

Kaden Croker straightened up, ready to be chosen. Ariel Beck also gave Wren her full attention.

'Francesca has indicated a champion of the Bowl and Doily Spider totem.'

After a moment of confusion, all eyes turned to Elsie Sloot.

She rose quickly and awkwardly, said, 'I accept,' and then tried her best to be invisible.

*

Mr. Croker insisted on escorting the champion, and soon an entire questing party formed around Elsie. Kaden, because he wouldn't suffer to be left behind, and Ariel, because her parents insisted, joined. Both brought their spiders. Nestis

Moises, the best healer in the village, joined at Wren's behest.

And so the party set off, and was soon near the base of the Mage's Tower. The tower stood by the lake, in a field of tall grass. It was separated from the woods by a group of old, abandoned buildings, which rotted among overgrown azaleas and birch saplings. The cracked, weedy pavement was covered with the bodies of birds.

Ariel gasped.

Elsie thought she might vomit, then the feeling passed. Meanwhile, Croker stepped forward and turned over the body of a blackbird with his toe.

'Ew,' said Ariel.

'Don't touch them,' said Nestis. 'You'll get sick.'

Elsie tried to speak, but no sound came out. She cleared her throat and tried again. 'Come on,' she said. 'Let's go to the base of the tower, and see what Dot tells us to do.'

Elsie took a step, but seeing that no one made a move to follow, turned and reviewed the group. Croker scoffed and shared a smile with Ariel. Nestis, perhaps eager to get the excursion over with, picked up their pack and forged on. Elsie gratefully followed. Croker decided then that he should reach the tower first, and jogged ahead.

*

By the time the whole group gathered at the tower's foot, Croker was already poking the edifice with a stick. The surface of the structure appeared solid enough, but gave like viscous mud. Meanwhile Mr. Croker complained that his head was starting to pound, and excused himself to sit and drink some water.

'Well? We don't have all day. Let's see what your spider has to say,' he called to Elsie.

Elsie set down her homemade spider coop – a little tube of reeds and cheesecloth – and coaxed Dot with a gentle cooing. She sweetly asked the spider to vouchsafe her instructions.

Croker and Ariel mouthed the ridiculous word 'vouchsafe' a few times, barely suppressing their amusement. Nestis noticed, and clicked their tongue. The teenagers, caught, suddenly busied themselves with their own spiders.

Gradually Dot emerged and climbed a stalk of grass.

'Climbing,' said Croker. 'Obviously. The spider's telling us to climb.'

'Yeah, because that's worked before,' said Nestis.

'Look what she's doing,' said Elsie. 'I've never seen her do this.'

Dot had reached the top of the grass shoot, and was standing on her tiptoes. The spider looked for all the world like she might lick a tarsus and hold it up to gauge the direction of the wind.

'Coop her, quick!' said Nestis. A desperate edge in their voice made Elsie jump. After a little fumbling, Elsie had Dot secure in the coop.

'She was getting ready to balloon,' explained Nestis.

'Balloon?' scoffed Ariel. She had Jewel, her marbled orb-weaver, out of her crystal-pendant carrier. Ariel had made it a kind of idle game to let Jewel spin a thread down from her hand, which she would periodically gather up with a twist of her wrist. Elsie smiled to herself; as careful as Ariel was to appear cool and confident, she had no idea how silly she looked. The hike through the woods and the breeze off the lake had whipped her hair into a frayed mess. With her orb-weaver yo-yo and her hair standing up, she was a rare sight.

'She was about to spin gossamer and catch a breeze,' explained Nestis. 'Fly off somewhere. Migrate.'

'I know what ballooning is, thank you,' said Ariel.

Elsie looked down at her coop, which she now held in her lap as she sat on the ground. 'Dot? Were you going to leave me?'

'It can't be true.' That was Nathaniel Croker, back again. He levelled a no-nonsense gaze at Nestis.

'I know what you're thinking,' said Nestis, nodding sadly.

'The oracle – '

'Follow the spider's instruction,' repeated Elsie, mechanically.

'The council won't agree to – to a migration!' said Mr. Croker. He looked like he was about to panic. He was rubbing his temples furiously.

'I'm not saying we're supposed to abandon the village, Nate!' said Nestis. 'I'm just saying Elsie's spider was about to balloon.'

'What else could it mean?' Mr. Croker shouted.

'It means the old lady was lying!'

That was Ariel. She had struck everyone dumb, and now had the floor. 'I'm head of the class in arachnomancy. I've studied Old Miss Pattengale's entire oracle journal, all of Francesca's seven-point patterns, all of it.'

'Go on,' said Mr. Croker.

'I didn't see anything in Francesca's orb about Elsie Sloot.' She turned to Elsie, and added, 'no offense.'

'Maybe she made a mistake,' said Mr. Croker.

'Maybe you're not the arachnomancer you think you are,' Nestis suggested to Ariel.

'Well,' said the teenager, 'I brought some silken rope for lashing and climbing. I really think this is a job for an orb-weaver totem. Why don't you let me and Jewel try, Mr. Croker?'

'It's not Mr. Croker's say,' interrupted Nestis. 'He may be council-leader in the village, but here? He's just a self-appointed chaperone!' Nestis took a deep breath. 'Sorry, Nate. That was out of line.'

'None of us are feeling ourselves lately,' he said, wiping his face. 'And you're right. It's the champion's say, I guess. Elsie?'

Elsie was still sitting on the ground cradling her spider coop. She tried to think what Wren would do in this situation. Finally she said, to Ariel, 'All right.'

Ariel pulled a fortune's worth of silken rope out of her pack. She laid the skein aside, then carefully selected a piece of driftwood from the lake shore, and set it down just so, a few feet from the tower's wall. She extended her hand, and allowed Jewel to drop, on her silk thread, down to the driftwood.

It didn't take long for the orb-weaver to find a prominence, stand on tiptoes, and point her abdomen upwards.

'Ariel,' said Nestis, with the same urgency as before.

But Ariel put up a hand to silence the healer. 'Don't you think I know my spider?' she said. 'Jewel's species only balloon as spiderlings, anyway, and – '

The spider let out a fan of gossamer, and took off. Ariel cried out, wheeled around, and grabbed at the air with futile desperation.

'Which way? Did anyone see?'

Only patient and watchful Elsie had seen. 'She went straight up,' she said, with wonder.

Ariel turned to Elsie and nearly spat. 'You knew this would happen. You wanted this to happen!'

'No, Ariel!'

Nestis and Mr. Croker both moved to put themselves between the two girls.

Meanwhile, young Croker had been putting two and two together, in his own way.

'Look, Ariel, I'm sorry about Jewel, but – but if Miss Wren did lie or whatever, and both of you – with your web-spinning totems – are just going to lead the village to abandon our land, well, you know, maybe the true champion has a jumping totem. Dagger can't balloon. He doesn't spin.'

'Well, why not try,' said Mr. Croker. He folded his arms and reconsidered his son. Maybe the boy had more political sense than Nathaniel realised. 'That is, if Elsie says so.'

'Dad, that's not what I'm saying. I don't need her permission. Wren's a liar. I'm the champion, not Elsie Sloot.'

His father dropped his arms, and shook his head in

disappointment. 'You may find it foolish to question Miss Wren's arachnomancy,' he warned.

'Let him try,' said Elsie, with sudden forcefulness.

Croker at first met this with a mocking sneer. But his expression changed as he remembered what happened to Ariel. Anyway, it was too late to back down now.

'All right,' he said. Soon he had lowered his birch and leather spider coop to the ground. Dagger emerged in due time.

'Well, what's he doing, champ?' asked Ariel.

'Exactly what he should be. Acting like a spider.' Croker said as he stretched his hamstrings. 'You girls had it all wrong. Expecting your spiders to perform some magical semaphore or something. Follow the spider's instruction – you're overthinking it.'

Croker watched Dagger, and did kata-like forms from Jumping and Reflex training. Some footwork, a couple of open-palm jabs. Then he picked up Ariel's driftwood, and approached the surface of the tower wall.

'My spider teaches me speed and a light touch. I think no one's climbed the tower yet because they haven't been quick and light enough.'

Croker pressed the stick into the wall, and put his full weight on it. The surface gave, at first like foam rubber, then like honey. But the driftwood didn't get stuck. Croker let go, and it simply slid down to the ground.

'Now look,' he said. He examined the texture of the wall for footholds, and sprang up. More in the manner of a gibbon than a jumping spider, he climbed about ten feet up, then scrambled back down.

'I think I can do it,' he said, panting. 'I just have to stay ahead of the melt.'

'Kaden,' said Mr. Croker, shaking his head. He looked up, to where the tower disappeared in the low layer of nimbus clouds hovering over the valley. 'You're not superhuman. Even at your quickest, how far up could you get before the wall started to give?'

'Even without the weird melty stuff,' said Nestis, 'it's a sheer climb. I mean, you're very clever to notice that speed is a factor in the melting. But – am I going crazy here? – have you ever climbed a cliff before? Without climbing gear? It's not like you could even anchor pitons or set up a fixed line.'

'I'm with Nestis, son,' said Mr. Croker. 'Use your head.'

But Croker was tired of being underestimated. He jumped. First his father, then everyone, called after him as he scrambled up the tower. He was thirty, forty, fifty feet up.

His stamina started to give out, and one hand slipped.

'Damn it, you'll fall!' shouted Nestis.

'No,' said Nathaniel. 'He'll be okay.'

The slip-up had scared Croker. He had grabbed the wall, good and tight. This of course meant his hands and feet sunk into the oobleck covering the tower. He was able to keep his face out of it as he gradually slid down to the ground.

Nestis checked him for injuries and instructed him to drink water in small sips. While the senior Croker and Ariel half-heartedly massaged Kaden's ego, Nestis approached Elsie and sat next to her.

'What do you think? What do we do?'

'We follow the instructions of Dot,' Elsie said quietly.

'We abandon the village?'

'No, Mx. Moises,' said Elsie. 'I know why Wren – I mean, why Francesca chose me. I'm the smallest. And the lightest. Look at Ariel's hair.'

Nestis was confused, but obeyed. Ariel, hunched over her fingernails as Croker's dad was giving the two of them a heart-to-heart, still had no idea that her hair was standing up every which way.

'I don't get it,' said Nestis. Their hair was curly and oiled down; Elsie's was tied back in a tight French braid. The Crokers kept their hair close-cropped. Elsie rubbed her head, and a few strands came loose and stood up.

'See? Don't you feel it, in the air? Whatever made Dot and Jewel want to balloon?'

Elsie stood up and approached her rivals.

'Ariel, you were right: we need your silk. And Croker, you were right, too. We were overthinking the oracle.'

They stared at her.

'May I?' Elsie indicated the loose bundle of silken rope.

'You're not going to make a cobweb and catch the mage when he comes down for a piss, are you?' said Ariel.

'Shut up for a second,' said Croker.

'Nice hair,' said Elsie.

Ariel noticed the state of her appearance, and tried to smooth her hair down. She only made it worse.

Elsie helped herself to the silken rope.

'Mx. Moises – you were talking about mountain-climbing stuff before. Do you know how to make this into a harness?'

Nestis did. They started wrapping one end of the silk rope around Elsie's hips. Meanwhile, Elsie took out her folding knife and started fraying the other end of the rope.

'Are you crazy? Do you know what that amount of silk costs?' Ariel whined.

'What's the plan, young lady?' asked Mr. Croker.

'She's going to balloon,' said Nestis. 'That's it, isn't it?'

Elsie smiled at Nestis broadly. She let go of the frayed strands of silk, fanning them out.

The strands lifted into the air.

To the astonishment of Ariel and the Crokers, Elsie's feet separated from the ground.

The elder Croker looked to the sky, as though he might

catch a glimpse of the Mage himself waving a magic wand.

'I don't like this,' said Nestis. 'How will you get down? What if you drift away?'

'I don't think I'll drift away. I think this force that's lifting me comes from the tower. And I think this force is what's hurting the village.'

Elsie realized she was too heavy, and removed her jacket and her shoes. She handed them to Nestis, and began to rise gently.

'Take care of Dot,' she said.

'I will,' said Nestis. 'Until you're back.'

'Tell my parents I love them.'

'You'll be back,' said Mr. Croker.

'Either she's brave, or an idiot,' Kaden whispered to Ariel, as Elsie disappeared into the clouds.

Goodbye, Spider

Jackie Taylor

You stop after we've crossed the main road and tell me that it's OK, I don't need to walk you right up to the school gate from now on. Thanks, but no thanks, you say, in your eight-year-old, old-fashioned way.

Ok. That's fine, is what I say back. But what I really say (inside) is No. Not Ok.

You're dressed as a spider. Of course you are. And off you go and you turn and wave before you disappear round the thick, hedgy corner by the gate.

Goodbye. I wave back and pray that in the dark, hidden corners of the school you'll find your friends. The sort that look after you, have your back, stand up for you whatever/whenever you need it. Proper friends, not like the school-gate Mums who can exchange a look and raise an eyebrow, both at the same time, and without moving a single muscle. Superpower or what.

Please find friends. This is what I always pray, or something like.

So there's no need to walk you right up to the school gate any longer. Ok. That's fine. I'm guessing that I embarrass you – a bit (a lot). Or you want to be alone (I get that. Me too.). Or you want to protect me (no need. I know already that school = terror).

And off you go and turn and wave, and you're dressed as a spider. Of course you are, because that's the costume I made. I offered you tiaras, and wings, and pink, and silver, and shiny, but you wanted black and spider, of course you did. So cheap fake fur that sheds all over the laminate and ta-da! Drumroll. Off you go. And I'm proud-stroke-terrified, as the other kids in twos and threes and fours and more stream round you, my lone spider. You turn and wave from amongst the princesses and pirates in their beautiful costumes, bought from shops. And you, shedding small tufts of black fake fur all over their polyester.

Your spider thing – it makes total sense from when we lived in the van and we used that wildlife haven aka shower block. Peeling whitewash and completely open to the elements, more or less. We made stories about the spiders, do you remember? Our van more like a nest, and you and me, wrapped in blankets, making stories together to fill the stretched-out nights. I knew everything about you then.

It's so different now they've moved us to town, and the flat with a bedroom each and a hallway between us, and double-glazing that separates us from outside. And who knew that school isn't just your kid going to school, it's shed-loads of other stuff too? Baking, dressing up, making things, there's always something that you don't want to do, and I don't want to do, but it seems like we have to do. To fit in. Sort of.

I gave your spider costume a tail. Why not?

So I'll just cross the main road with you from now on, and watch. I'll always pray that in the dark and hidden corners of the school you'll find the other spiders, that you'll find each other, that they'll be your friends, that you'll protect each other. This is what I'll always pray, probably, or something like.

You turn, and strands of black fake fur fly up and catch the sun. You're inside a silver halo, and you wave out at me.

Spider Circus

Patty Tomsky

The flea circus folded in the fall of 2001. I was dancing to Missy Elliott when I figured out what I would do next. I was able to dance alone a lot in the single dorm room I got every year thanks to a diagnosis I made sure the Dean of Students received. The paperwork was frank, yet elegant, completely false. I'd found some letters online from a famous psychiatrist of some renown, his specialty a condition that caused me to need a single room. Not wanting to pay more for the privilege, not able to, I'd manufactured a letter, some authoritative-looking medical files. Photoshop rocks.

I'm sure I look infested with fleas as I shake and twist in my own special dance for no one, it's bliss – even as I see the blinds on the window, next down, drawn and seeming to purse in disapproval. Then: the new idea.

Of course, the flea circus was a fake. It was a mechanical curiosity, no more, with the 'performers' nothing but the viewers' imaginations, oh their silly, collective glee at the spectacle of nil: fleas on teeter-totters; fleas pushing tiny balls up tiny hills, a baby Sisyphus crushed by his own hubris, punished by his arrogance and determination, both.

I'd used the flea circus to bankroll tiny niceties not afforded me through my loan, through the measly scholarships I'd cobbled together, for one semester at a rich kids' school in the centre of a cold city that hardly ever saw the sun. My little-kid-sized sombrero with the pink and lime green thread work and sequins was set out on an empty table next to the circus, in the corner of the Student Centre. The sombrero slowly filled with one dollar, two, underneath the sign that said, 'Fleas don't eat air, drop a dollar for flea kibble.'

These kids can spare it – their $200 shoes tell me so as they slap on the tiles of the student centre, as they tumble in from the cold, like puppies. I'm standing, watching the webs grow in the corners as I am talking to one or the other of them. There's always slush smearing the black and white harlequin of the tiles here – this city gains its renown from snow, and winds, blowing to flush and redden cheeks off the lakeside, sand frozen in whorls and spikes, a sculptured scream.

'What's next for you?' The tall girl with the jolly demeanour asked me. I sat at my table. The flea circus had already left town in the dumpster behind the dorm. Empty crushed boxes from cases of ramen cradled it to its grave in some landfill somewhere, I confess I shed a tear.

The table was empty now, but I claimed it until I had the chance to build my spider circus. I didn't want someone to take it from me – one of the do-goody-two-shoes clubs around campus for homeless people or euthanised pit bulls.

I'd been noticing the lace out of the corner of my eye for some time, and when the jolly girl spoke, she interrupted me wondering why I didn't see any spiders' bodies form those curtains of grey, filmy web. They must be there somewhere. Every once in a while I caught a black spark of movement and climbing legs, a flash of mandible, the warm roundness of the arachnid thorax, somehow foul and fecund all at the same time, gleaming in the fluorescents, a tiny, noxious fruit at the end of balletic fronds of legs like eyelashes.

I'm angry when the jolly, sporty chick speaks to me, partly because I want her and I know she couldn't want me – anaemic, angry, shabby me. I thought of all of the indignities of losing my few dollars a week from the flea circus, money I spent on vodka and gooey Cinnabons from Schlotsky's on the quad, and I wanted to scream.

'What's it to you?' I was surly to this girl, who'd never left me a cent, I was sure, but watched the flea circus slack-jawed like some farmer's daughter.

'I loved your circus,' she snuffled a nervous giggle in response, 'I miss it, sorta.'

Her vowels were both long and flat in that Midwestern way, a bit of Norway in their music.

'I'm gonna make one with spiders next,' I said before I could stop myself. It was her shyness made me say it, the humble duck of her neck, a pitiful curtsey.

'No way!' She lit up.

'Way!' I said, mocking her, but she didn't react to the false, snotty chirpiness of my response, thought my manufactured enthusiasm was matching her own.

'How you going to do that? There's a way to mechanise fleas but spiders are too big, aren't they?'

What a fool, I thought, but said, 'Oh there's a way. Trust me.'

'You should patent it then,' the girl said. 'I thought flea circuses were over and done with, except for the ones you see on those nostalgia shows on T.V. I live with my Grandma and she's always watching those shows and I never thought to see a flea circus in real life until I saw yours.' As she spoke, her chestnut ponytail swung behind her like a metronome. Her sweatshirt and shorts were both emblazoned with the name of our university, and the pale blue and white colour scheme made her complexion more florid in contrast. I saw she was flabby not healthy, not really sporty at all, with a convex paunch evident even under the thick jersey of the sweatshirt. She stopped herself, as if she knew she was blathering nervously. I shot her a smile.

'Well then it's your lucky day,' I told her. 'I'm going to let you help me make my spider circus,' I stood up and put my palms flat on the table between us.

'Really? Aw, that'd be great!' Her ponytail swung even more vociferously. 'When?'

'I'm in Hawthorne,' I told her. 'A8.' Shit, I thought. That was dumb. No one knew where I lived. Except for maybe the people on my floor and I never talked to them.

'Cool! When, I mean what time?'

'Midnight. Tomorrow,' I said, just to goof her a bit. She didn't skip a beat and it occurred to me this girl was as lonely as me.

'Cool! Cool! Do you, uh, need anything? Like um, soda or chips or that?'

I thought for a second that she'd bring me a covered dish, a hot gooey casserole that church ladies from the region trucked in, their stock in trade, along with green jello 'salads' and sausages beading grease on a plate.

'Nah. I'm good. You like beer?' Most of the snots I went to school with here had no idea I was five years older than them. They'd have been friendlier if they knew I could legally buy booze for them.

'Sure! Yeah!' she said, and I thought her ponytail would spiral off her head and into the air, she was so thrilled. 'See you then, I guess?'

'What's your name?' I asked her.

'Karla,' she said. 'Karla Knauss. Pleased to meetcha – ?'

'Theo,' I told her. 'Just Theo. Like Lourdes. Or –'

'Or Cher! Yeah that's great. Cool, welp, see you then, thanks, Thea!' She turned with a wave.

'It's Thee-OH!' I shouted at her back, but she disappeared in the throng of students they'd just let out of their 10:30 class.

I was pissed at myself. I couldn't cancel – she'd not even left me her cell. I finally figured I could look her up on the campus portal, get her email there and cancel. I calmed down after that, enough to almost enjoy the way the festooning webs grew and changed in the corners, finally draping down over the laughing students' faces as they walked with their fake friends, drifting into their open mouths and eyes completely unnoticed and unremarked, the most natural thing in the world. A natural order of things, like rich and poor, sad and happy, alone and together. They couldn't notice the contagion of spinning fibres around them because they were blissfully unaware of any context to their lives, to their privilege, to the endless access only money could bring. I wondered for once if Karla saw it too – I know she probably felt it. The way the air around certain cliques of kids was rarefied, not with expensive perfume but with expectations well-met with events unfolding, as smooth and clean as an emerging thread shot out and into the air to stick in the perfect corner of the room, festoon it with promise, dead, rounded, wrapped insects dreaming themselves to death, when they wake, dizzy, nearly bloodless, to see her fanged slavering approach.

After coding a game for one of my classes, I'd become ravenous. I chomped down a cheeseburger from the vending machine down the hall in the study room. A few nerdy guys were there, using flash cards to study for a chemical engineering course I'd tested out of. Hawthorne was the science dorm, but only one other kid from my hall was a comp-sci like me. The rest were earth science or bio, pre-meds I called 'preemies' in my head they seemed so inexpertly formed, embryos undercooked and sent shivering out into life.

I nodded at the guys and they goggled back. When I got back to my room, I realized why – my tank top was thin, and the study room had been chilly. These co-ed dorms had their irritations – men being the biggest irritation of all.

I typed *Knauss, Karla* into the student directory and nothing came up. Then I did a search on Google and even sent $5 to one of those 'My Life' sites that had a likely suspect listed:

Klauss, Karla Age 20 Relatives: Gertrude Klauss Karla Klauss Simon Klauss Elsa Klauss (D) and the name of one of the little podunk towns down the interstate a ways, a town where the fertilizer chemicals fought the manure molecules in mid-air to an uneasy, miasmic truce.

Once I dialled the number, I heard a male voice say, *hello?* And before I could finish, 'Is anyone there? Speak up, dammit!' I snapped into my charming young thing mode – crotchety old men were a specialty of mine. Like spiders, they were deliciously easy to predict – if you knew the shape of web they'd likely weave. Then you knew all their habits and how to best remove them from their homes so they couldn't drop down on your head in the darkest hour of the night. If you were really, really smart like me, you could keep them alive and move them into a circus.

Old men were quantified by where they lived – if they still lived in their homes, where they had been young men, they tended to retain a grand-poohbah attitude, equal aggro and patronising, sometimes too loud; well, nearly all of them spoke too loud. This kind was speaking too loud because he didn't want to get a hearing aid – vanity. Some couldn't afford good ones or any at all. They apologised and almost whimpered, 'What? What?' when they could not understand. This type, the guy on the phone, was choleric and angry and would never ask anyone to repeat themselves.

'Yes!' I shouted, a smirk on my face at the powerful feel of standing in my empty dorm in my underwear,

'Is Karla there?'

'Karla Senior or Junior?' the old man asked.

'What?'

'Karla SEN-YUR er Karla JOO-NaYER.' He seemed to think loud enunciation would help.

'Uh the woman who's about twenty?'

'That's Junior,' he said, and dropped the phone on some type of hard surface. He must have been a spry old dude because I heard his voice move far away at a solid clip, yelling 'Junior! Phone!'

Karla's voice. Quiet. Sad. She knew what this meant. Or thought she did.

'Hey,' she said. 'Theo?'

She'd heard me after all. I don't clam up much from nervousness, I mainly do it from selfishness and arrogance – *why do I need to talk to the likes of them?* Now, I was appalled at the croak that emerged.

'Yes. Theo. Hey about later on –'

'Oh, okay that's fine, I have so much homework anyway, hey, did you take Psych? Mrs. Reagan?'

'Yes. Last semester,' I chuckled. 'Sorry, kid,' I told her. And stopped myself from saying more.

'She sucks – the worse we do, the more work she gives us. The whole class has Ds,' she whined in my ear. Paused.

'I thought I'd order in some pho – what kind do you like?' I said. Something about the graceless way this girl was reacting to me was charming. Her idiocy was almost mesmerising. I pictured her standing on one leg, leaning against the doorjamb of a doorway in a goldenrod coloured kitchen, her grandfather grunting over his pipe and newspaper in the handkerchief-sized study through the door from the kitchen, not four feet away. Listening.

'I don't know what that is,' she said, but her voice was softly ecstatic.

'I'll show you. And Karla?'

'What?'

'There aren't any spiders.'

'What? There aren't?'

'No. And there weren't any fleas.'

'Really?'

'Really.'

'Never.'

'Never. It's a trick. A joke.'

'Ohhhhh–' she breathed out. Her voice got stronger. 'Well, that's okay. That's just fine.'

'You sure?' I was smiling bright and wide and thinking of the Miller tall boys in my mini fridge and the Vietnamese pho delivery that would come by at seven or eight, and the way she would discover the miracle of the new, the real and the sustaining right in front of me, in my little room, as she sipped a simple soup from the other side of the world.

I thought how she probably didn't know how to be unkind or snobby or entitled. How she'd been a little girl, walking through the chicken house with a basket, spiders, big barn spiders, watching from their webs, warm cows breathing all around, and reach down to find a small, perfect egg underneath the feathers of a hen that barely stirred from sleep.

'So, see you a little earlier if you can?' I asked. Something was uncurling in my chest, cracking open and unravelling.

'How does seven sound?' She was confident and strong, I'd found her, I'd hunted her down, I'd teach her to eat pho, I'd play her Missy Elliott, I'd sit in Schlotsky's with her beside me and we'd split a Cinnabon and a coffee, and cheerfully split the check, holding hands on the way out and not caring we'd just spent our last five dollars in the world.

Stowaway

David Mathews

Limestone and Old Red Sandstone, they are made of, the Blasket islands and the Dingle peninsula that is their mainland. Through the window the woman searched for them, but even with the telescope it was no use. A mist had come in from the Atlantic and she could not make out which bit of south west Ireland was which.

She turned back and read again. It was not the last paragraph of the book, not quite, but she read it twice more. Had the writer been with her, she would have hugged him, this man telling not of the geology of the Blaskets, but of the lives lived there.

I have written minutely of much that we did, for it was my wish that somewhere there should be a memorial of it all, and I have done my best to set down the character of the people about me so that some record of us might live after us, for the like of us will never be again.[1]

'Personal call, Roberta. Okay to take it?'

It was okay. She did not get many of these nowadays. Jobs like hers had become too common to make you a celebrity.

'Dr Bruce, it's Terry here at First Direct, about your flat. I've got down that the tenant is going to be there a year, okay, but how long will you be away in total? I just want to put a note for the renewal next year.'

'Three years,' said Roberta.

'That long? Going somewhere nice, if it's alright to ask?'

'Well, Mars.'

1 Tomás O'Crohan, *The Islandman*

Roberta ate, thinking of life on Great Blasket, and how one of their fresh eggs or a pint of beer would go down well right now in this quiet spot between Earth and the Moon.

Although ships had been whizzing to Mars for well over a decade, it still took around three days to reach the Moon. No-one seemed anxious to speed up space. On earth, planes, trains and automobiles were slicker than ever. But you still ambled to the Moon at not much more than Earth escape velocity, the cost of greater speed being excessive, Roberta supposed.

On the *Tereshkova* she was a passenger, content to let the automatic systems pilot her to the *bike sheds*, the station in lunar orbit from where the Mars ships headed off and the local landers descended. It was to have been called *Grand Central,* but the Russians objected, and, to spite the Yanks, went with the Brits' nickname.

Besides, 'Old Mr Putin would have liked bike sheds, behind which you make deals, yes?'

Roberta was the only passenger, the four Italians who were due to join her having been caught up in some political shenanigans.

From her work on the basalt surveys of several lunar 'seas', Roberta was used to the way in which you were kept an eye on during space travel. She had learned to ignore it, so much so that, for a while at the start of this trip she had felt truly alone. Since then, however, she had had the sensation of company, of being watched in a keen way, her movements tracked. Had she seen a face outside the window through which she had looked at Ireland, she would not have been surprised – in a manner of speaking.

She shrugged. *Bother it, Roberta. Come on, let's see what's in the book box.*

Most ships carried a book swap. You could call up pretty much any book online, but space travel was tedious, and if you wanted to lose yourself for a few hours, nothing beat a grubby old paperback. Skilled readers could use the lack of gravity to read without having to hold the book.

The volumes in the box were usually ancient. She rummaged. Machiavelli's *The Prince.* The Chinese loved this, and bet madly on being able to quote from it, in Italian. *Pride and Prejudice,* natch. *À la recherche du temps perdu* in French, English and Russian. You read Proust on the return trip from Mars, not the outward. Few books after the mid-2010s for some reason, only Boris Johnson's seminal *Diplomacy*, and short stories by an obscure author born, like Roberta, in Cardiff.

To see her through to the bike sheds, however, Dr R S Bruce, PhD, FGS, CGeol, MBE chose Elmore Leonard's *Rum Punch,* his 'new bestseller' from 1993. One, because it was set in Miami, which she had come to like; and two, with no one around to talk to, she fancied the quick-fire dialogue.

The eerie feeling crept on her again. She turned, though she knew no one could be peering over her shoulder.

'Course adjustment, Roberta. Five second burn. How was lunch?'

'Five star, Bill. That blue cheese will have me hallucinating.'

'Does it for me, Roberta.'

It was not her brain that Roberta doubted a few minutes later, but her sight. A display across the cabin looked fuzzy. Rubbing her eyes and cleaning her specs made no difference, and everything else was clear, just that blur. Moments later she was laughing. Just as an Atlantic mist had obscured Dingle Bay, here the culprit was a cobweb, or rather a grey and white striped spider one centimetre wide, with six dark, steady eyes.

'How in the world did you get here?' said Roberta.

Spaceships were meant to be free of bugs of any size, from bacteria to insects. You did not want them on a voyage, and you were not meant to leave them anywhere you touched down. But as travel to the Moon and its bases became routine, cleaning services that once were the realm of skilled technicians were put out to tender, and standards slipped. You found smeared windows, sticky switches, hairs and nail clippings, human detritus which, from the DNA, could serve as the passenger manifest. But a spider, that was something.

'You're not quite the Alien, but do you bite?'

Checking whether Spider was liable to bite a person – or poison her – was not easy. Roberta was astonished at how many kinds of spider came up on her search. Even stripey ones with six eyes.

Any spider might bite you, Roberta found, but in most cases the venom suited the spider's prey rather than its predators, and her little guy seemed to be not too much of a risk.

Why she did not squash it, however, she could never fully explain.

Maybe she credited Spider with pluck. How brave of it to undertake this monster journey – and how many times?

Maybe she felt an urge, unfamiliar in her life of dedicated research, to nurture another being. Certainly, she spent some time deciding what Spider could eat, bluebottles being off the menu.

Maybe she was reluctant to exterminate any companion, given that there was no other within 100 000 miles of her.

Maybe because she had kept chickens as a child, but not had a pet since.

Maybe simple fellow-feeling, the two of them, Spider and Roberta, being so comprehensively out of their natural environments.

Whatever the reason, Roberta called Bill in Houston to say that she had had not so much a problem as a dilemma. She had resolved the dilemma, and now sought advice on how best to get Spider back to Earth.

After Spider's safe return, by which time Roberta was on her way to Mars, a zoo in Texas gave the not-so-tiny bug a home, and crowds flocked to see her. She was a sensation. Schoolchildren all over the world adopted Spider; the little arachnid got into in *Playboy* magazine as Pet of the Month; *Spiderblog* was voted the educative site of the year in Russia, Brazil and Australia.

In Britain, where the interest was as great in Roberta as in the spider, 'Spiderwoman' was too obvious for several newspapers to pass over. 'Little Miss Muffet' in a space suit featured in at least a half dozen cartoons, while the tabloid headlines 'BUG-EYED MOONSTER' and 'SPIDERS ROCK FOR GEOLOGIST' gave the fuss a traditional Fleet Street feel. 'Woman geologist (53) finds spider on way to Moon' was the driest summary.

Only *The Scotsman* displayed a proper feeling for history. It picked up on something you spotted in this story long ago, of course you did. Their headline?

'Robert-a Bruce and the Spider'.

NOTE: The first spiders went into space in 1973, when Anita and Arabella were asked if they could spin webs on Skylab. They discovered they could.

With Great Power Comes Great Responsibility

Helen Morris

For Conrad, Oscar and Leo

Everyone always wants to know my origin story. Always. 'How did you get these powers?' they ask. 'What made you the 'man' you are?' Well take a seat. Perch just there. And I'll tell you all about it.

It was a rainy October night and I was there late in the lab, round the back of the glass beaker storage shelves. Minding my own business. Just pootling around, you know. Tidying a few things. Tying up a few loose ends. Fixing some bugs. I don't bother the scientists. They don't bother me.

Suddenly all hell breaks loose. There are alarms going off, red lights flashing, shouting, and with a great clang the big door with the rubber seals starts swinging shut. People running everywhere. Things get smashed. I hide behind the shelves because I have NO IDEA what is happening but none of it looks good.

And then the door closes with a hiss and it's silent. A good long twenty seconds of total silence. I catch my breath. And then I hear it. Slow, steady, footsteps and I see the tall skinny one, Brian, that's his name, walking heavily towards the big door. He's older than most of them. Always talking about his 'retirement'. He doesn't look too happy. But I'm not surprised, that door is the only way out and it's clearly not opening any time soon. I watch him from behind the glass beakers. I don't want him to see me. But he does.

He sits down slowly. His back pressed against the door. His legs bent. He takes off his glasses and wipes his face. Then he looks at me. 'Don't be afraid,' he says. 'It's nice to have some company. It's not like there's anyone else this side of the door.' He beckons me. 'Come on,' he says and so I come out slowly.

He pats the space on the floor next to him. 'Come over here,' he says. 'After all we're in this mess together. You and me. Well, you and me and the radiation leak. We're the only ones this side of the door. Everyone else is the other side. I mean that's how it's supposed to happen. With a leak. But it's not exactly how I imagined Monday going. I won't make bridge. Not after this.' I edge forward slowly. He looks pale. Unwell. These scientists never look great to be fair. But he looks even worse. So I move even closer.

And that's when it happens. He slumps sideways, I think he's fainted. And as he slumps sideways, his dentures fall out his mouth and they literally bite me. On my abdomen. These radioactive-saliva-covered dentures. THEY BITE ME! I've been bitten by a radioactive man.

Getting bitten by a radioactive man called Brian when you're supposed to be the epitome of stealth and cast fear into the hearts of humankind with a simple scuttle is embarrassing. Embarrassing. What kind of self-respecting spider gets bitten by a man? Honestly. The shame.

I skedaddled out of there back up behind the glass beakers as quickly as I could, I can tell you. Nursing my pride. Nursing a row of teeth marks. Luckily, we spiders are tough. So I recovered. Sort of.

Because I wasn't simply a spider anymore. Oh no. There were new things I could do. New powers. Man powers. I found, for example, that I could access the lab ethanol, drink it, tell the other spiders I loved them and then dance like a maniac for a good forty minutes before collapsing asleep wherever I was and in whatever position. Other spiders were awestruck! I also discovered that I didn't spin a web anymore. Oh no. I span a web sofa. Yep, you heard me – a web sofa. No balancing on finely spaced silken threads for me. Actual soft furnishings. Kapow! Spider chillin'. I also can't resist fried chicken. And sides. I know it's not good for me, but it's just so tasty. That's the human in me. And, the best power of all – bad puns. That uniquely human superpower that we spiders have so long looked at with envy. I can now make other spiders groan and roll ALL of their eyes. I am a spider pun LEGend. Geddit?

So yeah, that's me. Man-Spider they call me. I quite like it. Man-Spider. And Brian? Oh, bloody Brian is fine. Full on rescue Brian got. Back in the lab six weeks later, joking about setting the Geiger counters off. Talking about retirement. Dentures back in.

Brian is fine.

And I am Man-Spider! I mainly use my man powers for catching villainous neighbourhood spiders. By lulling them into a false sense of security with my amazing puns. And then getting them drunk on my special web sofa. They say I'm a hero. But I just like to use my Man powers for the good of arachnid kind. It's not everyone who gets bitten by radioactive Brian. Got my own song too. I'll sing it for you:

Man-Spider, Man-Spider
I can drink twenty pints of cider
Eat fried chicken, supersize
And some coleslaw and some flies

Am I powerful? Listen fam
I got bitten by a radioactive man

With eight legs comes great mobility
With great power, comes great responsibility

The Aspects of Arax

Maria Kyle

My cell is eight spans wide by eight spans broad by eight spans high: the propitious ratio of a sacred cube. Three walls are baked brick, simmering red, and coarse to the touch: the fourth is missing. In its place is a clumsy lattice of iron bars arranged in the rough pattern of a web; a tribute to Her. The workmanship lacks delicacy and finesse – nothing like the exquisite metalling I knew in the Agate Temple and cannot hope to see again – but then so does everything about this place. They are not subtle, the Oblivion Chambers, and neither are the gaolers who patrol them, gliding silent as blind, monstrous fish in a sunless temple pool.

There are no windows, so I cannot tell the time by light or darkness, sun or moon. My body knows when it is hungry; when it must eat, sleep, weep, speak. Otherwise it is as dumb as Bahel the Tongueless, guardian of the gates of dream, which are barred to me down here. Night after night I lie staring at the changeless absolute of the dark, straining my eyes until I can almost envision the holy constellation of Arax floating above me, her eight limbs spread in welcome and benediction.

I count her gifts east to west, in an arc like the sun's across the sky (the sky! How long since I saw it?) Sometimes it soothes me to contemplate the pairs: it reminds me of when we were children reciting the Lullaby Prayer with Mama, beginning with the Cup in Her right foreleg and the Corn in Her left, through the Ring and the Cord, the Scroll and the Sword, to the Sun and the Moon. Sometimes I pluck at the rough bars until my nails jag and bleed. Often, exhausted, I pass from the waking world into a deeper darkness. But what is sleep without dream?

When the morning comes – and by morning I mean a surly gaoler carrying a smoking rush torch, to light the sconce in the passageway to my cell – I scratch another mark on the wall with a chip of fallen brick. There are seven lines of eight now: my time is growing short. My breakfast is frowsty water and a dull mess of meal-gruel in an earthenware bowl. As I mouth it I try to remember the ruby tang of grapefruit between my teeth; the crispness of feather-thin apple-slices on my tongue; the honeyed sourness of goat's curd.

Once I ate like a goddess – or a queen, at least. The offerings are sacred to Arax, but what She does not want (and what could She want? She owns the universe) belongs to the Priestesses once the sun slumbers. Forah and I were the most senior, the most devoted, the most devout of Her handmaidens. In spite of this, or perhaps because we knew ourselves to be protected and indulged, chosen daughters of the Many-Mother, we gorged ourselves witless on this bounty, especially at harvest feasts and on Her eight sacred Versaries.

Her birthday and deathday, the twin hinges of the year, saw us stuffed with crocodile steak and peacocks' tongues, hysterical with palm wine, until the Low Priestesses had to haul us from the altar, still screeching in laughter: or sometimes scratching, spitting, scything at one other, a welter of drunken limbs. If we'd each had eight arms like the Goddess, on those nights both of us would have used every one to strike at her sister. Such is love and family. Such is the brutal bond of blood.

After these excesses, one of us would wake as normal in our shared bedchamber, alone, while the other – usually she who had screamed the loudest or fought the hardest – would blink to life lying on the cold obsidian of the altar slab, with a head dry and heavy as a roasted ox. I have felt that slab beneath me an armful of times, at least as many as Forah has. In eight days' time I will feel it again. My blood slows and sickens at the thought. My sister will be there, of course, in her ascended aspect of Arax, known as Bydra: Forah no more, she embodies pure power. The goddess speaks through her now, and She has commanded my death.

The torchlight is orange and sullen, rippling lakelike in unseen gusts of foul air. Through the grid of bars and shadows I can see only the blank wall of the corridor, down which echoes sometimes screaming, sometimes silence. I cannot say which is worse.

The food passes through a hatch in the heart of the iron web, where a swollen black blob squats, crudely moulded to represent the Goddess. Her fangless mouth becomes a slot for a platter; her all-seeing eyes spyholes in a metal mask, behind which my visitors stand when they do not wish me to know them.

They ask for predictions. They ask for prophecies. They sue for favours and forgiveness. They plead for the lives of their sick children, the deaths of their enemies, the flourishing of their crops and livestock. They demand of me the secret to swelling their coffers, their herds, their wives' bellies. Sometimes they beg in whispers to know the future or the past, what death feels like or how the heavens spin: for I am Kyat, the Goddess's second aspect, now; which is why I am kept dark. I see and know all things already, for I embody Her knowledge just as my sister wields Her power.

Yet still I cannot dream. Perhaps my head is too full? Forah – Bydra – has an answer for that.

Some days I tell my visitors the truth, and some days nonsense. Some days I speak a language they know, and some days I improvise one to amuse myself, babbling a waterfall of syllables they cannot catch or interpret, but are awestruck by. I laugh and rave, but never weep: weeping is a privilege of privacy, for myself alone. Some days I say nothing from the moment the torches are kindled to when they burn out; only close my eyes and lace my eight fingers in prayer over my shaven skull. But on those occasions, I am not fed the day after. And even an earthly aspect of the Goddess must eat.

Some days my sister comes, and those days are the worst.

*

Mama is dead now. We both salted our lips with a chalice of her blood-in-water at the funeral, the highest honour the Temple can bestow. But when she lived they called her the Spider Mother, for live twins are a wonderful rarity, and mirror-sisters the luckiest of all. Well; until they are lucky no longer. As I came out (the eldest, the strongest, already bellowing like a cow in heat according to Mama) and they made to cut the cord, the midwives were astonished to see a tiny hand wrapped around the living vein like it was a rope. While I bawled on my mother's sweat-slick belly, they coaxed her out: my passenger, my second half, and worked her waxy limbs and blew into her blue lips until she coughed and was truly born.

I had half-killed Forah in the womb, it seemed; crushed and deprived her with my foetal greed, but she survived nonetheless. Just. She survived and grew strong and fast, until we were as tall as each other and as alike as two blades of wild grass. But she never forgave me that early attempt on her life. She is certainly exacting her revenge on me now.

As soon as we had been washed and named, we were consecrated to the holy order of Arax: the Sovereign Aspect even declared our mother an honorary virgin so that she could nurse and raise us in the Agate Temple. And Mama became known as the Spider Mother, because she gave birth to eight limbs: though waking we were jealous rivals, in sleep each sought the other in the cot, ending in a tangled embrace: two heads, two bodies, eight arms and legs. Spider Mother, too, because she spun a web around us of protection and mystery. And Spider Mother because her venom could burn, her silken words trap and bind. Either or both of us would have been assassinated by envious sister-nuns a dozen times had it not been for Mama.

When she died we knew we were alone again; or as alone as twins can ever be. And we became afraid. The Aspect, Bydra-as-was, was an old woman, weakening daily. We stopped speaking to the others and whispered only between ourselves; there was nobody else we could trust, there was treachery in every trembling thread of the Temple's fragile web – yet nobody dared harm us while the Aspect lived. Then one night she ascended to the stars, leaving behind only her empty moulted body, just as Arax sheds her shell each century so that the universe may grow larger. The night after she was wrapped in silk and burned, the trials of succession began.

*

I read in the Temple library once of a sea-creature called a nurse shark – perhaps mythical, perhaps real, though the name must be ironic if it truly exists. This animal has two uteruses, in each of which she nurtures a score of embryos. These feed and grow, uncurling like buds, swimming in the salty darkness of her twin wombs, until one reaches the size of a handspan. This strongest child, in order to feed itself and grow yet greater, begins to consume its siblings. The smallest first, of course: the runts and the stunted, the slow and the weak, those which would have no prospect of survival outside the mother's body. But as it grows larger, so does its prey. Its sisters and brothers must begin to fight back. What a bloody drama played out in the black belly of a shark! And finally, after a gruelling labour, the victor emerges triumphant from its mother's body, chief cannibal with the ocean as its kingdom, born a murderer with a taste for blood.

And in the meantime, inches away, slithering silently from the nurse shark's second womb, its twin does exactly the same.

They did not tell, these close-written pages, what happened to the bloody twins if they ever met; whether they swam by instinct in opposite directions; whether one of the offspring was always born late or early, so as to prevent them destroying each other – but I wondered fiercely at the time, and now I know everything – or everything but – I know. If those sibling sharks ever meet they will recognise each other. And one of them will die.

*

I think I began to know too much, even back then. The trials of succession, I understood at once, were the wombs of the nurse shark. One womb was the arena for those who struggled to embody Kyat, the Knowledge-Keeper; the other nurtured those who would become Bydra. We did not eat our opponents, but each novice or priestess as she was defeated was banished from the Temple into the secular world, where the humiliation of marital bondage awaited. The victorious Sovereign Aspect, whomever she turned out to be, would recruit sixty-four new handmaidens for her new reign. How could she trust the old ones, after all? The tradition stretches back more than five hundred years, eight by eight and eight again, and has kept an uneasy peace in the kingdom for all that time.

True, there have been dreadful despots and terrible famines; appalling betrayals and destructions, earth-saltings and city-sackings: every great kingdom suffers such things. But there has never, never been chaos. Besides, the trials of succession are ordained by the Goddess. Who are we mortals to protest? We must only pray.

The gifts of Arax are multiple and mighty
we are humble and grateful
eight fingers offer eight prayers
to the Water-Finder
the Corn-Grower
the Husband-Eater
the Many-Mother
the Knowledge-Keeper
the Sword-Wielder
the Sun-Bringer
the Moon-Weaver
We are obedient and devout
The gifts of Arax are eight blessings upon us
Who are we? We are nothing. This is what I now know.

*

Eyes the mirrors of mine stare narrowly at me from behind an iron spider-mask, pupils glittering silver and black like haematite. It is not a looking glass nor a dream, but as dreadful as either. It is my sister, hiding her face. (Why? She is omnipotent and I am omniscient!) It is two days before we would traditionally face one another in combat, and one day before she has ordered my execution as a sacrifice to Arax on the obsidian slab that we drank and dined off together for so many years. Forah, as the new Bydra, has invoked the privilege of her power as no other Sword-Wielder ever has, to rid herself of the only true rival she's ever had. As I knew, even without the benefit of becoming the Knowledge-Keeper, she would.

'Even if I didn't know everything already, I'd know you by your eyes,' I tell her, as she draws her absurd black cloak closer about her, 'and if not by your eyes, by your hair.' Gleaming black waves of it fill the cloak's hood, impossible to hide: it is unmistakably a priestess's hair, and we are the only two priestesses left.

She frowns but does not step from behind the mask. 'As for hair, whatever did you do with yours?'

My own voice comes back at me like a sour echo, a mockery, a distorted mirror. I remember our mother weaving identical eight-stranded braids into our hair for our Belonging when we were no more than two spans high. We'd locked our fingers in each other's throughout the ceremony, exalted and terrified, and when, after, we tried to let go we could not: our fingers had cramped together. Memory is like air to me now, all around, utterly clear.

'I saw you would shear it at the sacrifice, so I decided I might as well do it myself.'

This is a lie. I did it because a shaven skull gives nothing to grab hold of, whereas four feet of hair most certainly does. I do not intend to lie down on the altar like a trussed beast. She will see that like the nurse shark, I have teeth too.

All hatred is love in a mirror, I think, as I watch the disappointment fizzle in her eyes. Perhaps Arax brought more than eight gifts when She spun down from the cosmic web: perhaps love and hate come not from within us, but from Her? This is what I think, but what I say is 'Why are you here, anyway?'

A tiny sneer. 'Don't you know, all-seeing Kyat?'

I keep my expression perfectly neutral. 'I know. I want to know if you do.'

'The custom is that the Sovereign grants the Sacrifice a last wish the night before her execution. As you know. And so I am here.'

Reluctantly, grudgingly, boiling with fury at the indignity of it – but yes, so she is: inescapably here.

'I suppose there are conditions?' I sigh.

'It must be something I can grant you from within your cell,' she says. Her hands are washing one another nervously, like a fly's. 'A visit, or a meal... a letter, an object... a book, perhaps?'

Such little things, for someone so appallingly mighty. Yet she is still afraid I will think of some cunning loophole through which I can escape or conquer her – that I will outsmart her and like the genie, leap from my bottle. Forah is so afraid I feel it throb from her like heat from a tile roof. What a terrible destiny she desires, to be so alone, for the rest of her lifetime. Whom can you trust when you have the power of life and death over everybody? Whom can you love?

'No thank you,' I say, as I knew I would. 'I will have a dream, please.'

'A what?' Oh, the forgotten pleasure of being surprised.

'I haven't been able to dream since I ascended, I don't know why. Unless it's Bahel's feud with Kyat over the Moon-Bridge seven hundred years ago. But I need you to command him to let me through the gates tonight. I need to dream.'

She hesitates, suspecting a trick or catch where there is none. Power without knowledge is truly a dangerous combination. The worst manifestations of Bydra have become terrified tyrants, executing swathes of perceived enemies as their inner circle constricts around them. But what could be more harmless than a dream?

'Very well,' she says, and turns away rapidly, her cloak aswirl. 'Tonight you will dream.'

And tomorrow, I think, watching her shadow slide along the passageway, *I will die. Or you will.*

*

That night I dream, uselessly, of being an infant again. I must have been very young indeed, for I was almost helpless when Mama picked me up and buried my warm bald head in her breast. When she laid me back in my cot and took up my sister to nurse, I felt cold and abandoned. My tiny fists spread and clenched like starfish but could grasp nothing. I began to cry, that heart-cracking hiccup cry that only the smallest infants know. I was utterly bereft: of warmth, love, company. I felt keenly, hopelessly, that I was as distant from any other creature as a star in Arax's leg was from the earth.

Then Mama put my sister down beside me. I thrashed furiously, and brushed her sleepy hand. She was warm and silky and smelled of milk. I, who could barely control my body, somehow rolled closer. She wriggled vaguely and snuggled against me. It was as though her skin became mine, her flesh my flesh. Our limbs folded over one another's, soft origami. Four arms, four legs, two bodies and two heads.

Spider sisters.

Sicarius

Carolyn Robertson

Lydia's palms were sweating. The Stakeholders of Sicarius Marketing Solutions were seated at the enormous table in front of her, waiting. Lydia's was the final pitch of the day. The company was moving away from traditional direct marketing strategies and embracing digital; they were hungry for a rebrand to reflect their new direction. Papers were shuffled, coffee cups drained, pens tapped. The clock struck three. Lydia clicked the remote and her presentation launched onto the screen *Web solutions for a changing world.*

As soon as she'd finished the board were on their feet. Claps and cheers erupted around the table; the CEO abandoned protocol and gave Lydia a hug. But not everyone in the room was happy. Anthea, Lydia's immediate boss, was seething. She'd presented her rebranding pitch earlier in the day and considered it watertight. She'd handed Lydia the task of mocking up a rebrand assuming her junior would do something inferior. Anthea simply wanted to showcase her own talents and provide the board with an illusion of choice. She'd given Lydia only four days to prepare her pitch, it had taken Anthea a month.

The CEO addressed the excited boardroom.

'Anthea, what can I say other than that you are the master of your trade and you've certainly nurtured genius here. My first thanks go to you, for your efforts earlier today and for being such a magnificent mentor.' The applause rang around the room and Anthea feigned an appreciative smile. 'However, I think we are all in agreement that Lydia has encapsulated our new *digital first* direction in the most inspiring fashion this afternoon. Your in-depth analysis of how we can penetrate social media and expand into new territories is absolutely the right way forward for the company.' As the clapping continued Anthea slunk out of the room.

Lydia primed herself for the inevitable fallout from her boss, but was unnerved when none came. Anthea was seemingly immune to any ill will. She helped ensure the rebrand got off to an efficient start. She gave Lydia useful tips and advice, sat attentively when Lydia wanted to lead in meetings. Anthea shared her knowledge of great freelancers for the TV ad, and web developers for the digital rebrand. Lydia began to believe that Anthea had simply come to accept that her ideas were superior. She developed a haughty air around the office and felt vindicated when a deputy director's role was proffered that gave her almost equal rank to Anthea.

The final part of the rebrand involved hunting for an image to go with the new logo. Lydia spent days trying to find something eye-catching, but didn't feel she had come up with anything strong enough. She looked over the images that Anthea had used in her unsuccessful pitch; one caught her attention, a striking six-eyed Sicarius spider emerging from a hole with the caption *don't bury your talents in the sand.* Lydia was impressed with the photograph and wondered how Anthea had obtained the spider shot. Reluctantly she went to see Anthea at her desk.

'Where did you get the spider photo for your pitch from? I can't find anything decent on any of the stock sites.'

The faintest smile twitched at Anthea's lips, she looked up from her desk and beamed at Lydia.

'Oh, she's mine.'

'The spider?' Lydia couldn't hide her incredulity.

'Yes. I've always had a thing for spiders, she's a fascinating pet. Sicarius Terrosus, she's a sand spider, I got her just after we started up the company.'

'Eurgh, really?' Lydia balked. 'Christ, I'd rather have something I could at least stroke.'

'Oh you can, she loves being handled. I brought her to the office for the last pitch shoot. She loved it, a real star on the day. Are you thinking you'd like an image for the campaign?'

'Yeah, but, not a sand one, I was thinking more webby,' Lydia said.

'Ah, she doesn't spin, I'm afraid, more of an ambush kind of girl. But...we could easily add backdrops with Photoshop afterwards.'

'Yeah that could work,' Lydia said.

'Great, just let me know when you want me to bring her in.'

Lydia kept her distance on the day of the shoot. The spider was larger than anything she'd encountered in the corners of her living room. Its six eyes unnerved her. She watched as Anthea delicately placed the spider in different positions in front of the green screen. She seemed so at ease, cooing and stroking the hairy beast. Lydia was captivated. The photographer clicked from different angles, props were added for the spider to walk over or through and close-ups taken. At the end of the shoot Anthea carefully placed the spider back into its Perspex box and placed it on her desk. Lydia had the courage to move forward and take a closer look, she pulled up a swivel chair and was soon transfixed.

'How poisonous is she?' Lydia asked.

'Her venom's necrotoxic, but her fangs are too small to puncture human skin, maybe when she's a little bigger...'

'What do you feed her?'

'Crickets, locusts, anything that scurries across the sand at the bottom of her tank.' Anthea took a seat next to her.

Lydia peered even closer. 'She's actually quite crab-looking. I mean the legs, they're …oh look, she's burying herself!'

Both women watched in silence as the spider began to deftly fling small legfuls of sand over her body. Within seconds she was barely visible. Lydia was entranced.

'That's incredible.'

Anthea lowered her voice to a whisper. 'She can lie in wait like that for weeks. Waiting, waiting, patiently waiting and then, when something disturbs her…snap!' Anthea clapped her hands together.

Lydia jumped in shock, she flew back in the chair, and her foot caught the edge of the desk. The Perspex tank toppled to the floor spilling sand and spider. Lydia screamed as she felt something hot and needle sharp pierce her ankle.

'Keep still!' Anthea made lightning work of recapturing the spider and placed her back in the tank. Lydia was shaking and she had curled herself up in the chair. Anthea placed a hand on her forehead. It was cold and clammy.

'She b…bit me.'

'I doubt it. You're probably just in shock,' Anthea said.

Lydia slowly lifted her ankle off the seat to inspect it. Two tiny drops of blood beaded just above the bone. Anthea placed a reassuring hand on Lydia's shoulder.

'It's just a surface wound, she would need much longer to inject any venom.'

After several cups of sweet tea and repeated assurances from Anthea, Lydia felt well enough to leave the office.

Lydia returned to work with nothing more alarming than a headache the following day. Her manner was brusque and dismissive towards Anthea. She was anxious to go through the shots from the previous day and find the perfect image to complete her campaign. She shuddered at the stills when they flashed up, enlarged on her screen. Her hand moved instinctively to the spot where she'd been bitten. As she rubbed, she felt a coarseness at her fingertips. Strange, she'd only shaved the day before. Her leg hairs had sprouted a week's growth within only forty-eight hours. Lydia put it down to a change of temperature and season and made a mental note to pick up some disposable razors on the way home.

Anthea passed by Lydia's desk at lunch time.

'Great to see you're okay. I'm nipping out for a sandwich, can I get you anything?'

Lydia didn't even bother looking up.

'Yeah, can you grab me a chicken roll?'

'Chicken?' Anthea asked.

'Yeah chicken,' Lydia replied, pounding at her keyboard in irritation.

'But I thought you were a vegan?'

Lydia stopped for the briefest of moments.

'I think I'm low on protein. Chicken's fine thanks.'

Lydia devoured her sandwich at her desk but later regretted not moving around as her back had started to ache. She decided to stretch and head for the loo. It took her several attempts to stand up right and she cursed the office chairs for their poor ergonomic design.

Lydia grabbed her handbag and hobbled across the office. She'd been sweating and figured she'd need to freshen her make-up. The ladies was empty. Lydia was about to push open a stall door when she caught a glimpse of herself in the mirror. She turned fully and faced the glass. Her forehead looked oddly swollen. She ran her fingers over several bumps that had appeared. Was it hives? The lumps were strangely symmetrical and squashy to touch. Lydia leaned closer towards the mirror and noticed something else, her skin had an odd grey pallor and her cheeks were covered in small dark hairs. Panic began to rise as she realised that the hairs spread from her cheeks and down her neck. Lydia pulled at the buttons on her shirt and stared at her chest, horrified.

Surely this was just a bizarre hallucination? Lydia backed away from the mirror. Maybe she was over tired? She'd put so many hours in recently, perhaps her mind was telling her she needed to slow down? Lydia took in a deep breath and closed her eyes. She would breathe deeply until she felt calmer and then… what was this? She could still see? Things were blurry, but coming into focus, six eyes blinked open.

There was no mistaking what was looking back at her from the mirror.

Barefoot

David Mathews

Spider needs food; autumn frosts are on their way.

Cyril must get on. He hates to be distracted. This morning he has splattered two troublesome bluebottles on the shed window. Spider could have done with one of those.

The fly? She is ripe with eggs, desperate to get a good host on which to lay them, flying madly, buzzing.

*

Spider's web is the sixth she has woven in Cyril's shed. There is no telling what brings on the man's spates of tidying and cleaning. In August it was the Olympic boxing in London. Nicola something? The young woman's energy and poise lifted him out of the doldrums, so Cyril told his son. Out went the piles of old newspapers, in came a shiny, new kitchen bin; the grass got cut, and, in the shed, away went empty paint tins and Spider's old web by the window. 'Sorry,' Cyril said, to spiders at large.

Exiled from the window, Spider built her replacement web across the shed doorway, top right corner, where the warped door no longer fits. Rather than repairing the door, in really cold weather Cyril blocks the gap with a cloth, but having to bother with that is a month or so away.

How did Spider know that this would be a productive spot? The rays of light between door and frame in the middle of the day? Or was it the air that flowed through, sometimes one way, sometimes the other? Spider's last babies were sucked into the world by this route one gusty day. No tragedy, they were about ready.

Tucked in behind the door jamb, motionless, Spider waits.

When the bluebottles took no notice of Cyril's 'Bugger off', Cyril swotted them. Tasty though the flies might have been, Spider did not follow their scent, not being a wanderer. She does not regret missing out. She is a spider, a speckled, brown, hairy spinner of silk, whose nature is to wait and wait until moving is worthwhile, at which point she takes advantage, and fast.

Cyril, conscious of autumn passing, gave himself a target this morning: a white bishop and three pawns to be turned on his lathe before lunch. He finished the black pieces two weeks ago, in cherry, to give them time to darken before Christmas. He is now working in apple, the palest sapwood he could find. He turns it slower than the cherry; too fast and it is liable to scorch, he reckons. Close to midday, the pawns are done, and the bishop is under way. Patient work for a retired old jazzman.

The lathe's motor whirrs for long minutes, accompanied on and off by the pitch of a gouge, sharp against spinning wood. When the machine pauses, the only sounds are Cyril's mutterings as he measures his work, and a buzz, fainter than that of the dead bluebottles. But these sounds – mechanical, human, insectile – determine nothing; no more do occasional outside noises, not cars, not the council's leaf gatherer swishing along the pavement, not the telephone in the house. Spider waits, and Cyril turns his bishop, regardless.

For Spider does not hear Cyril's wood-cutting or swearing, having no organs for such a purpose; and for Cyril, the only sounds reaching his brain these days are those he generates himself, his 'fucking tinnitus'. Why, then, those bluebottles? Ah, the problem was not their buzzing, but the care they took to tickle Cyril's ears. Had he been a cow or horse he could have flapped the wretches away while he carried on, but he had to break off from the lathe to swat them.

(A new fly has appeared. She does not know how much she is chancing, circling Cyril, with his rolled-up newspaper to hand.)

Without his hearing, Cyril has learned that the world vibrates. No longer can his ears tell him when a gouge is losing its keenness or that his veteran lathe needs attention. That intelligence must come through his fingers. Cyril's great uncle Fred, whom the guns at Ypres had deafened, learned to place a hand in front of the radio – correction, the *wireless* – when music came on.

But, for Cyril, Evelyn Glennie was the one, playing in bare feet, the better to feel the music. Now Cyril hardly ever wears shoes, not at home, and amuses himself distinguishing passing cars from buses and trains and his own dodgy heart. He does worry, though, that with all these vibrations the house might fall down one day.

Now, had he given Spider any thought, Cyril might have been jealous of her. Those legs of hers are not hairy just for show.

Four weeks ago, when a beetle took to the air seeking somewhere richer in food than the shed floor, and crashed into the web, it was through the hairs on her legs that Spider learned how big, how dangerous her prey was, how to approach it, how best to paralyse it. Now the beetle hangs, wrapped in Spider's silk, drained of nourishment. Nearby, the wings of a desiccated moth are forever outspread, Spider having known the creature for what it was even as it thrashed itself deeper into entanglement. And how did Spider eat the innards of these captured beasts? You do not want to know, trust me.

Had one of Cyril's bluebottles evaded the newspaper, and made for the gap in the doorway, Spider would have known exactly what she had been served for lunch. But speculation is not spiderly. Once she has set her trap, Spider deals only with what comes, not what might have been.

A breeze through the doorway shakes Spider's web, but does not summon her to action. No more does the vibration of Cyril's lathe get her moving; all morning Spider has felt it, but she has learned that it represents neither food nor threat. She waits.

If she were a person, an all-knowing concierge, as it were, she might pass the time with a magazine. *Knitting and Crochet? Web Designer?* But aside from more genes in common than you might expect, Spider is as unlike a human as you could wish, unless, in their stillness, you count coarse anglers. No notion of good and bad, of success and failure, of yesterday and tomorrow. Simply whatever instincts equip her to survive long enough to breed the next generation.

While Spider waits, Cyril examines the bishop as it spins, lines up his next cut.

A fly lands on his hand that holds the gouge. Cyril blows at it, the fly transfers to his hair. Cyril shakes his head.

The fly tries for the garden, and is thwarted by the window, five, six times. She orbits the lamp above the lathe. Window again, lamp, window, lamp. She needs to lay her eggs.

Back to Cyril's hands, nose, ears and neck, the smell of sweat and dead skin irresistible, taking over from the lure of light.

She bothers the man, tests his patience.

Cyril stops the lathe, picks up the newspaper.

The fly has no notion of retaliation and anger, but she knows when moving shapes require evasion, and is too nifty for the *Daily Mirror.* Three times Cyril misses the fly. He turns back to the lathe.

Spider waits.

Beyond the shed, in the house, soup simmers, and bread is sliced. As a cheese is unwrapped its smell interests a black and white cat. Preparing the lunch is Peter, Cyril's son, the father of the chess player to whom Cyril's work is dedicated.

(Cyril taught his granddaughter chess when she was five. She gave the pieces individual names, even the pawns, and was as loyal to each one as other children were to their dolls or Lego figures. Black pieces were girls, even the bishops and knights, though not the king; white were boys. Now, at fourteen, she is way past Cyril's playing level, but she will never outgrow the figures she has asked him to make.)

Lunch is ready.

Peter leaves the kitchen by the garden door, shooing the cat from the kitchen. He walks across neat grass to the shed, opens the door.

Spider feels the increased draught, is aware of greater light, but does not tense or move. She waits.

Peter is a tall, broad man, who all but fills the doorway. Around his head the sun makes a halo. He mimes a knife and fork as Cyril looks up. Cyril responds with a soup-eating gesture, and laughs. Peter makes a face; dad joke.

The fly heads for the new bright light, to the side of Peter's head, top right of the shed doorway. No belief in freedom, just compulsion.

Spider moves.

Interspecies Peace and Love Song

Guy Russell

The Old Beam's Nook was heaving like a dead mammal. Closter on bass; Charlotte, with the most elaborate drum-kit ever seen in this corner of the world, up on her back legs and using the rest to pound the tubs, but Tara stole the show on harp: an extraordinary self-made wonder-machine with super-silk strings that produced a sound so aching, so searing, you just wanted to spread your wings and lose yourself in it. They looked good too, dangerous and sexy: Tara flaunting her long, hairy legs; Charlotte displaying her muscular black sternum; Closter with his unfeasibly large pedipalps.

The crowd that night was unusually mixed: fleas giving it the pogo, salticidae jumping, bees waggling, normally uptight formicidae doing their line-dancing thing. A posse of moths jitterbugged in the light-show. And hordes of fellow diptera: all of them seriously buzzing.

Buzzing too much, I thought. Hot musos or not, these were rachies, after all.

I interviewed the band later, as arranged. Backstage, they had a pretty cool crevice, and were hanging near its entrance. 'Do you want to come a bit closer?' asked Tara. 'I won't bite.'

'I'm fine here,' I said. 'Tell me about your music. What are you trying to *do?*'

'The messages in our songs are about love, interspecies peace, and fighting arachnophobia... You look so fascinated by my harp. Come nearer!'

'No,' I said. 'It's fine. So tell me about the next single...'

'They always try it on, whatever,' I said to Terrie afterwards, over a meal at The Putrid Hedgehog. 'They see you're a dipt, they start thinking with their fucking chelicerae.'

'You've got to admit,' said Terrie, 'there's something unique about them.'

'The music's *shit*,' I said approvingly. 'But I do worry about the big diptera fanbase. I saw a couple of the crowd go back to their crevice... Do they think that's going to end well?'

'You're just getting old, Flynn. I thought they didn't eat their fans? Or hardly ever? I mean, unless they want to be eaten?'

'Yeah, I bet,' I said. 'No diptera *wants* to be eaten. That's rachie powertalk. But rachies definitely want to eat *us*.'

The next time I was assigned to them, they were at Behind The Shovel, a bigger venue with a even bigger crowd. 'Tara's so *dangerous*, but so *sweet!*' burbled one excitable gnat I voxed beforehand. 'Just because you're a rachie, just because you're a dipt,' fan-sang a couple of others to me evangelistically. 'Doesn't mean you have to hate them. Doesn't mean you have to nip!' A couple more, barely more than larvae, were alternately swooning and vibrating their antennae in a way I found quite disturbing. When the band came on, it was like a jam doughnut had fallen from Heaven. And I noticed all the love and peace posturing didn't stop the band doing a cover of *Inject the Venom*, which I'd always considered borderline dipterist. But the crowd, especially the young flies, chorused along madly. And OK: I admit I wasn't unmoved myself – but that was just the temporary magic of art.

'Thanks for the writeup from the Nook,' said Tara, afterwards. We were at the bug hotel, and it was quiet apart from a few ants clearing up. 'You really created a buzz for us. Especially among the diptera community.'

I liked the praise. But I wanted to pose some tougher questions this time. 'So how do you feel about your massive diptera audience?' I asked.

'They're beautiful! We love them!'

'But,' I pointed out, 'you do eat them, too.'

'Hey, that's just the System, man,' said Closter, looking hurt. 'We can't do a lot about Nature. Not till the Evolution, anyway.'

'Actually, I'm pretty vegan these days,' said Tara. 'I catch seeds in my home-web mostly. But sometimes some poor creature gets trapped, and panics, and injures itself so badly it's kinder to put it out of its misery.'

Yeah, right, I thought.

'We need to be more like humans,' said Charlotte. 'You know why they're Number One species? Sometimes it's better not to eat your mates.' She paused. 'Obviously, they're not great role models in other ways.'

I kept abreast of their career. Well, it was hard to do otherwise. The next two singles smashed all records and the album went totally barnwide. There were the usual troubles, of course. Stories about trashing hotels, disrespecting fans, getting into fights. Tara got briefly into acid – her harp-strings looked like funnel-web macramé till she kicked it. Charlotte briefly got religion, maybe out of guilt: Closter had fallen for her, and in the throes of passion she'd accidentally eaten his legs, but he grew some new ones soon enough.

By the time I caught up with them the third time they were massive. I mean, in every sense. Charlotte was twice the size. And Tara, already vast, had started exuding this royalty-scale presence. People were calling them the new Beetles. They'd sold out the Discarded Bathtub, basically a stadium setup. To a crowd going totally waspwindow, they rocked flawlessly through *Sculptin' The Air*, *Let's Make Eggs Together* and the other hits, and encored with *Interspecies Peace and Love Song*.

Interspecies peace and love. Right.

I had more trepidation this interview. While continuing to big up their artistry, I'd been pretty sceptical about their idealisms in my last piece. I'd mentioned phrases like *food chain* and *biological imperative* and *commercial hypocrisy*. And the megastars they were now, they no longer needed my middle-ranking pufferies. It might be tricky.

They'd taken over a nearby bar as their dressing-room, and I was due to do the interview there, but when I arrived, there was no one but a dozing security slug. Hmmm. Had I been snubbed altogether? The bar was all aluminium-shiny in the moonlight, and my pique was quickly dissipated by the glinting presence of Tara's harp hanging against it. It was so beautiful: shimmery, delicate, ethereal… I got a crazy urge just to brush it with my leg-tip and hear it do that extraordinary heart-breaking reverb. I checked no-one was around, reached out and flicked one of the strings. No sound. Perhaps it was turned off. I flicked harder, but blast. The string was sticky. I hoped I hadn't damaged it. I tried to withdraw my left-front leg, but doing so I touch it with my right, and that stuck too. Of course. What had I *imagined* the harp was made of? I was so *stupid…*

The instrument itself began moving. I saw Tara coming across from the bar. As she got nearer, her eyes lit up eightfold with hungry desire. Her fangs looked huge. She was so big. Hopefully it would be quick. At least I had my three hundred and fourteen children to continue the line…

'By the Spider Queen's Spinnerets!' spat Tara. 'Flynn! Are you *asking* to be eaten?'

'No! No!' I begged.

But it was too late. Tara's pedips were on me, holding me still. Her fangs came towards me – and past me. *It's* not *going to be quick*, I thought in horror, *she's going to wrap me for later munchies.* She began biting some of the strings around me, and rolling back others with her legs.

'You dipty scum,' she hissed. 'I thought you liked us. And now you're trying to ruin my career by making me eat you!'

I flapped frantically, even though I knew it would bind me further – and, to my utter astonishment, found myself in free air. I glanced rapidly back, to see a strange expression replicated in Tara's eyes, like she was struggling with something. I wanted to explain, to say thanks, sorry, sorry again, but instead I kept going, right out of the barn, just in case she changed her mind.

Across the Dark Void

KT Wagner

The spiders have multiplied. The constant tinny hum of the spaceship masks their noises, but they're there, lurking at the edges of my vision. I turn my head and they disappear into crannies.

Eradication is no longer a possibility, if it ever was. There are too many.

Over the weeks I've generated plausible excuses for my lack of action: *The loneliness stayed my hand. I had a concern I might compromise the scientific equipment.* Just yesterday I typed *The cosmic web mesmerised me* into the log.

All correct but none reflect the truth. Ground Control is not trustworthy.

I don't mention the distension of my cheek or the swelling that's closed one of my eyes or the heaviness in my limbs despite zero gravity. Maybe that's why I finally switched off the internal monitoring cameras. The second week out, I coated the camera lenses with dry lubricant, but a crawling unease whispered I may not have found them all.

The engineers didn't provide much room for a human crew when determining the cargo capacity of the space shuttle. The ideal pilot had to be under 65K, and 'relatively healthy'. The latter qualification meant free-of-plague-antibodies and it reduced the available pool to less than a dozen. All of us women. Conveniently, that suited the needs of the colony. They rounded us up and placed us in isolation. *Never too many baby-breeders.* My words, not theirs.

I didn't protest. On earth, exposure to the plague is only

a matter of time. Perhaps I could scrape together the cash to pay for drugs to slow the progression, but it only delays the inevitable. The shuffling, mindless, late stages of the disease don't bear thinking about. Nobody says it out loud, but the colony looks like the last hope for humanity.

I wasn't Ground Control's first or second choice. Maybe not even their third, fourth or fifth choice given the shortness of my remaining reproductive years. However, in the final stages of launch preparation, one of the loading crew bit the pilot's arm. By the time the security detail reached them, he'd gnawed through to the bone. They sent someone to retrieve their second-choice pilot from her cell and found her dead. Apparent heart attack. I now think the spiders had something to do with it.

Ground Control had released many of us the evening before. They found me as I trudged along the railway tracks, heading to check out a rental at a nearby trailer park. The previous night there'd been another meteor shower and I'd lain in a field to watch it. It tired me out and I curled up amongst the corn stalks and slept there. Odd. I never used to sleep very well.

This journey is one way. At first, I dreamed about those I left behind. Now, I barely remember their names.

In the event of my death, the sleeping pod is designed to preserve my organic matter. Ground Control didn't tell me this. I think the spiders must have. I trust them. I avoid the pod.

For the first two weeks of the journey, I slept in the pilot's seat. When I noticed a funnel web deep between a container labelled *mycorrhizae* and another labelled *cyanobacteria,* I took to securing my sleeping bag to the shuttle window.

The lights dim automatically every night cycle. I lie my face against the quartz glass, gaze into the expanse and wait on dreams. The smooth surface cools the heat in my cheek.

Contrived reality, a dry rustle of a voice in my head. It cackles.

The line between awake and asleep is no longer a certainty. The monitors might tell me, but I've stopped looking at them. The warning lights irritate me. I break a couple and an alarm goes off. My head pounds. Hours later the shrieking finally stops.

This might be the last supply run Earth manages. The plague spread faster than predicted and a cure is elusive. A group of scientists blamed the first meteor shower, but no one believed them. If they weren't all dead, they'd probably be saying, 'We told you so.'

A team of government scientists claim this ship's cargo will help address the terraforming issues the colony struggles with. The technicians sounded nervous as they explained this to me. Or maybe the microphones on their hazmat suits distorted their voices.

All around me are bio-containers of fungus, microbes, plants and insects. The spiders are particularly happy to be aboard.

I'm not a biologist or even a scientist, just an ordinary pilot. My job was to manually steer the shuttle past the dark side of Mars. I fulfilled my duty. Now I am mostly excess cargo. If I survive the rest of the journey – eight long months – my genetics could further diversify the colony, but I'm not interested in bearing children.

I don't think the colonists will be either.

A jab of panic accompanies this random thought – more and more are intruding – and I stretch my arms in an attempt to dissipate my anxiety. Space sick, nothing more. It will pass.

Orb webs edge the rim of the window, cloak the control panel, and mute the annoying auto-pilot lights. Funnel webs bridge gaps between containers. The webs glow a faint, iridescent purple. Or maybe the swelling around my eye is affecting my vision.

I've still not seen a spider, but their webs are everywhere. They're here and waiting.

The spun fabric of the universe unfolds around the ship. The blacks and pale beiges of the early weeks have evolved into kaleidoscopes of swirling colour.

Reedy, garbled voices twist through static bursts from the radio. Ground Control continues to issue their shrill petty orders. It wasn't difficult to rotate the receivers slightly away from both earth and the colony. The shift could be explained by the buffeting of space wind. Important, because Ground Control still has access to life support and other essential systems. Caution is best, for now. The spiders are working on a solution to silence Earth.

I pace around the pilot's chair, a kind of bouncy lurch that gives me something to do and perhaps staves off bone-density loss.

My fingertips brush a web. The strands are sticky and soft and not unpleasant. I run my hand through the silk and gather it onto my fingers.

Long ago, I lay next to grandmother and looked up while she spun fibre. I hold my hand out like a drop spindle, though I don't trust the memory. It feels new.

I rub the web-silk between my fingers, and the oils from my skin smooth and shape it into a narrow roll. My rhythm improves the less I concentrate. I spin a fine lavender-blue filament. Grandmother would be proud, except I'm pretty sure my grandmothers both died before I was born.

I gather more silk. Hours, perhaps days, float past. Calm replaces anxiety. Acceptance replaces calm.

#

Throbbing in my cheek brings me back to myself.

I hang centre-ship, facing the window and the galaxy. Earth is no longer visible, but one planet is less than insignificant among centillions of celestial bodies. A speck on a mote of dust.

The web is complete. A spun dreamcatcher. It connects everything in the ship to me, and through me, them. I wriggle and the movement shivers out along the strands.

My cheek burns and prickles. Seeking relief, I rub it against the web. A crawling sensation spreads across my face. I close my eyes. The pressure in my cheek lessens.

The receiver spits out an angry burst. I open my eyes. A few spider babies still scurry through the web, but most have settled in.

The shuttle continues on its journey to the colony. Our new home.

Web of Life

Elizabeth Hopkinson

Arachne is crafting her web. The crochet hook moves deftly under gnarled fingers.

Chain four. Double crochet. Slip one. Repeat.

Round and round, the circle grows. Loop into loop into loop. The silver thread sparkles.

Chain four. Double crochet. Slip one. Repeat.

Her fingers fly faster, faster. The need is urgent. When she began this particular web, she thought she had time. Time! Why did the goddess not grant her foresight along with a spider's body? Now she must spin and weave as she never has, growing the net ever larger. It must be wide enough for the catch she has in mind. Not one must slip through.

Chain four. Double crochet. Slip one. Repeat.

When the web is as broad as the shoulders of Atlas, she casts it, an ancient fisherwoman casting her net. It spreads from sunrise to sunset. Its silver chains pull taught enough to walk along, slack enough to bounce at a single touch. Retreating to her lair, Arachne waits. She closes her eyes, one leg extended to touch the last length of thread. Holds her breath. Will they come to her web? Will it catch them all? Has she toiled too long?

When morning comes, Arachne scuttles along the thread, feeling, checking. A pair of speckled wings. Stag-like horns. A shell of iridescent green. As she passes one form after another, her breath becomes easier. They are here. They are all here.

Names that once tripped so easily off the tongue. Fritillary. Stag Beetle. Southern Damselfly. Red Barbed Ant. Their ancient habitats shrinking, they fly to her for shelter. Silver-spotted Skipper. Adonis Blue. Hazel Pot Beetle. Where else can they turn but to the Spider Mother who will hold them safe in her silvery embrace?

And still they land, with a hundred little trembles. Arachne's web shivers to welcome them. Speckled Wood and Small Tortoiseshell. Jewel Beetle and Shrill Carder Bee. Arachne will preserve them, will save them from the hand of fate.

She will hold them safe, within the Web of Life.

About Arachne Press

Arachne Press is a micro publisher of (award-winning!) short story and poetry anthologies and collections, novels including a Carnegie Medal nominated young adult novel, and a photographic portrait collection.
We are expanding our range all the time, but the short form is our first love. We keep fiction and poetry live, through readings, festivals (in particular our Solstice Shorts Festival), workshops, exhibitions and all things to do with writing.
https://arachnepress.com/

Follow us on Twitter:
@ArachnePress
@SolShorts

Like us on Facebook:
ArachnePress
SolsticeShorts2014

Find out more about our authors at https://arachnepress.com/writers/